Doneraile COURT

The Story of the Lady Freemason

This Book Belongs to

....

KATHLEEN ALDWORTH FOSTER

Copyright © 2018 Kathleen Aldworth Foster
Library of Congress Registration #TXu002105295

First Edition

Published by Novel Development Books
Cover illustration by David R. Shires
www.theimagedesigns.com.

ISBN 979-8-9855430-0-1 (paperback)
ISBN 979-8-9855430-1-8 (hardcover)
ISBN 979-8-9855430-2-5 (digital)

Acknowledgments

Special thanks to:
David J. Butler, Provincial Grand Librarian and Archivist
for Munster Freemasonry
Doneraile Court and Wildlife Preserve
Ireland Office of Public Works
Mick O'Sullivan/OPW
Sheila O'Hanlon
Maureen and Richard O'Hanlon
Michael O'Sullivan/Doneraile Development Assn
The Creagh House/Doneraile, County Cork
The James O'Keeffe Center at Newmarket House
Ben Stocks, the St. Leger and Aldworth families
Christopher Knight/*The Hiram Key* Co-Author
Stan and Kathy Schuck
Mom Mom Kathleen Aldworth Schuck
Editors: Ella Jean Edwards, Poppy Kuroki,
Denise Painter, Claire Baldwin, Katie McGuire
All the Freemasons who helped along the way

Dedicated to my ever-supportive husband, Chris,
and forever curious daughters,
Elizabeth Aldworth and Mary Aldworth

Author's Note

This is the book I wanted to read when I first visited Doneraile, Ireland back in 2006.

But it didn't exist. So, as they say, I had to write it myself.

When I travel, I love to read historical fiction novels that take place in the towns I am visiting. I find I learn more about the people, places, and buildings—that might still be standing—than I do by reading the average travel guide. However, when it comes to this particular story…it's more personal.

My name is Kathleen Aldworth Schuck Foster. My middle name, Aldworth, is my great-grandmother's maiden name and it has always been special to me.

During a trip to the pyramids at Giza in Egypt for New Year's Eve 2000, a man told me I share the name with the first ever female Freemason, Elizabeth St. Leger Aldworth. The man gave me the book *The Hiram Key*. This is what first sparked my interest in the history and mysteries of Freemasonry.

Fast-forward six years, I was back in the Middle East. In August 2006, I was in Kiryat Shmona, Israel, a town that sits on a tiny peninsula of land that juts into Lebanon, covering a war between Hezbollah fighters and Israel. I was dodging daily Katyusha rockets and sleeping in an empty kibbutz while working as a television news producer.

I was preparing to leave my assignment early to meet up with my family in Ireland for a pre-planned genealogy trip to visit people and places connected with my recently deceased grandmother's relatives in County Roscommon.

Because of work, I hadn't had much time for extra-curricular research. So, during a few quiet hours between Katyusha explosions, I hopped on my laptop. However, instead of searching for our Roscommon family names, I typed in "Aldworth."

That's when I found out The Lady Freemason's initiation took place in County Cork. Upon our arrival in Ireland, our tour guide took us straight to Doneraile.

My interest in the life and times of The Lady Freemason grew from there despite the disappointing realization we are not directly related. I originally planned to write a non-fiction book, but because of the passing of three hundred years and layers of sworn secrecy, I hit several journalistic dead ends.

I realized to tell the story, it would be best to follow the lead of historical fiction authors like Geraldine Brooks, who says: "Historical fiction is taking the factual record as far as it is known, using that as scaffolding, and then letting imagination build the structure that fills in those things that we can never find out for sure."

Doneraile Court: The Story of The Lady Freemason is the outcome of that. I hope you enjoy the journey.

Kathleen Aldworth Foster
June 21, 2021

Prologue

November 1712

Everyone in Doneraile swore they heard a screaming banshee that night. The ear-piercing shriek echoed along the ancient Irish town's narrow cobblestone lanes, waking them with a jolt.

Babies burst into panicked tears; dogs barked frightened yaps. Mothers scrambled their children from their beds and hurriedly counted them, "Five, six, seven!" But no one was missing or dead.

Some of the braver men ventured outside to the cold streets, lighting the wicks of their handheld oil lamps, and clutching the collars of their jackets closed as they faced the fierce fall breeze. They glanced around, warily greeting neighbors, before retreating to the safety of their homes to calm their families and find their beds.

Dread loomed large and low like a heavy fog over the town for the rest of that night, for everyone knew a banshee only comes when someone is about to die.

1

The shiver-inducing scream reverberated in the ears of many who lay awake that night. Others were able to sleep but suffered nightmares of demons and monsters until the blessed arrival of dawn.

The morning was bright and cold, and the townspeople wasted no time gathering along Doneraile's main street to try to figure out the cause of that frightening sound.

"It was a banshee, I tell you!" cried old Mrs. Kelly her eyes wide as she clutched a baby to her chest, scuttling up and down the marketplace like an overexcited hen. "A banshee, I swear it! Nothing has made such a terrifying sound as that in all my long years!"

The others mostly ignored the woman's ramblings, though the word "banshee" induced trepidation in even the most courageous among them.

"Isn't everyone in my house accounted for?" whispered Mrs. O'Beirne to Mrs. O'Keeffe as they lined up outside the bakery. The sweet scent of baked bread and jam wafted through the air.

"Isn't everyone in my house, too?" Mrs. O'Keeffe whispered back, discreetly giving herself the sign of the cross.

Superstitious whispers rippled through the line

of waiting shoppers, and old Mrs. Kelly's babbling wasn't helping.

Everyone was frightened. It wasn't often something disturbed so many people in one night.

A little way away from the concerned bakery-goers, the daughter of Lord Doneraile glided past them, listening to the gossip. They didn't notice her disheveled hair, nor the bloodied bandage pressed to her chest, nor the small smile on her face.

Like everyone else in town, she too had heard the scream the night before.

She too would have thought it was unearthly… had it not come from her own mouth.

Chapter 1

THE LAST FULL MOON

October 1712

It all began a month before, on the night of the last full moon.

Bizzie St. Leger jumped awake in the night. The fire in her room had deadened to glowing embers. The pale silvery light of the moon was shining through her window and casting a ghostly glow on the polished oak furniture.

Shivering, the seventeen-year-old climbed out of bed, her toes curling as she stepped on the cold floorboards. The glow of a distant oil lamp flickered beneath her door, and the low, hushed voices of men sounded behind it. She pulled a shawl on over her nightdress, letting her auburn hair flow free, and cracked open the door.

The front hall of Doneraile Court was filled with panicked, chattering men wearing unusual short white work aprons along with their normal upper-class dress. Bizzie rubbed her eyes, her mind still cloudy with sleep, struggling to comprehend why her house was so full of men at such a late hour.

She gasped when she recognized the man in the middle, unconscious and covered in blood from a wound just above his heart. Her brother, John, was hurt. He often bled, the smallest of cuts causing him to do so profusely, but this time, he wasn't moving.

"What should we do?" hissed Arundel Hill. Arundel was a short statured bearded young man of eighteen who had once tried to court her. What could be seen of his cheeks above the whiskers were flushed pink. It was a look Bizzie had often seen on her brothers' and father's faces when they'd been at the whiskey. His whisper crawled up the stairs to the landing where Bizzie leaned over to see, her knuckles whitening as she gripped the banister.

"Here. Bring him here." She heard her eldest brother Arthur give the command, barely concealing the panic in his voice.

Bizzie watched in alarm as they carried John's limp body and deposited him in a moonbeam at the foot of the stairs, leaving a trail of his shimmering blood in their wake. Someone had lit several oil lamps, but the silver moonlight shining through the rosette window in Doneraile Court's front hall illuminated the spot where John lay, bright as daylight. His chest was bare. Blood was streaming from a cut just above his left nipple, down his side to the floor.

The men stood in a circle around him, the atmosphere heavy as they watched his unmoving body. One of the men was Bizzie's father, Arthur St. Leger Sr, the first Viscount Doneraile.

"Everyone, back away," her father told the group. Bizzie watched as her father untied his apron and knelt to cradle his son's head in his lap. He was trying to put on a brave face but inside he was kicking himself. How important was keeping the ritual alive if his son didn't survive to share it?

Bizzie watched as her father balled up his strange white apron and tried to use it to mop up the blood. Pressing and blotting… blotting and pressing, but the flow of the blood didn't change. The white fabric of his apron turned pink then red.

Bizzie's brothers Arthur and Hayes were also part of the group, watching, staring in disbelief. Just beyond them was the door leading to the room her father called the lodge room, the only place in the house Bizzie had never been allowed to enter. From her perch, Bizzie could see the door to the lodge room was slightly ajar, candlelight twinkling out from inside.

What had they been doing in there?

If not for their blood-stained clothes, one might have thought the men in their fancy dress were attending a royal court. They wore ruffled shirts and long buttoned waistcoats over breeches. Their shoes, some now dotted with crimson, were polished to a shine, and their long wigs were freshly powdered. The white aprons tied around their waists looked stark and out of place.

"Should we fetch a doctor?" Arundel asked, but his question seemed to fall on deaf ears. No one said a word, but Bizzie's chest loosened a fraction. John was alive.

"Why won't it stop bleeding?" muttered another man Bizzie could not see. Her view was obscured by the powdered wig of another man leaning over her brother.

"Arthur, what is wrong with your son?" Lord Doneraile did not respond.

"What's happening?" Bizzie's brother Hayes whispered to their father, trying to break Lord Doneraile's trance as he fruitlessly kept blotting with his soaking wet apron. "John bleeds. He always has. But this is so much blood for such a tiny cut, Father…"

A door creaked open to Bizzie's left and Lady Doneraile appeared in her lacy nightdress, her eyes widening in horror as she leaned over the balcony to see her son's body at the foot of the gleaming wooden staircase.

"Who is that? Is it John?" Bizzie's mother cried, racing past her daughter, and thundering down the steps, slippers slapping. The men scattered out of her way as she reached her son with a pained moan.

"Yes, madam. I don't understand why he's bleeding so much," said Arundel. "It's just a small cut."

"Yes, well, he bleeds a lot," Bizzie's mother snapped. "Hayes, my kit!"

Hayes sprang into action, shoes thumping on the floorboards as he ran off to fetch his mother's kit, strands of strawberry-blond hair escaping from his wig.

"Even so," Lord Doneraile's deep voice finally broke his silence, but not the worry etched on his handsome face. "A small cut like this…it shouldn't be such a problem…"

"You did this on purpose?" Lady Doneraile whispered, though it sounded more like an angry hiss. Lord Doneraile withered under his wife's reprimand.

He was saved by Hayes' reappearance, a mortar and pestle and a bowl of sugar and honey in his arms.

Lady Doneraile worked at remarkable speed, shooing the men away, mixing the sugar and honey vigorously in a bowl, and quickly applying a large dollop of the paste-like substance onto the tiny bleeding wound on John's chest. She tore off a piece of her own nightgown and applied pressure onto his skin, muttering to herself the whole time about clumsy boys and their silly games. It was not the first time she'd done this for her now adult son, and the Lady Doneraile feared it would not be the last.

Bizzie watched from the upper floor balcony, helpless to be of service. Her eyes slid from her brother and mother over to the slightly open door to the lodge room. She hesitated, worry for John battling with curiosity.

Curiosity getting the better of her, she started to move, making no noise as she did. She had memorized which floorboards squeaked, so she softly hopscotched around them until she reached the top of the staircase. She descended, her nightgown whispering around her legs. She tiptoed past the group huddled around her brother. No one took any notice of her, all watching her mother work, silence gripping the group. Bizzie glanced at

John on her way past. His mouth was slightly open, chest moving up and down as he breathed.

When she reached the lodge room, Bizzie stood on tiptoe and peeked through the cracked door, her heart pounding.

In the middle of the darkness was a small oval tabletop, illuminated by three burning candles. On the table was a thick, open book. Two shiny metal objects Bizzie couldn't identify were placed in the middle of the open pages, stacked on top of each other creating a diamond shape. What were they? She squinted to tighten her focus when the door suddenly snapped closed before her. Bizzie's eyes followed the hand on the latch up to see a tall man with a chiseled face and kind eyes. He wore a small, square white apron around his waist like the other men surrounding her injured brother.

"You don't need to see this," he said.

Shame flushed through Bizzie at being caught. She thought he meant the room, but he nodded toward John's unconscious form, where the blood clots had finally started forming thanks to her mother's work. The coppery scent of blood mingled with the too-sweet scent of Lady Doneraile's concoction.

"I've seen it before," Bizzie said quietly. She

looked up at the man. He was young, perhaps a little older than her. He pulled off his wig to wipe his brow, revealing a mop of dark hair he'd tied back like the bureaucrats did.

Catching her staring, he graced her with a soft smile, and the tension around her heart loosened slightly.

"Come," he said, taking her gently by the elbow like they were at a formal dinner, not in her home's front parlor in the middle of the night. As he opened the front door, the cold October air blew her nightdress up and over her knees, making her blush as she pushed the billowing material down. The young man pretended he hadn't noticed as they stepped outside together and asked, "'So, is it well-known your brother is a bleeder?"

The question surprised her. Most gentlemen introduced themselves when they spoke to a lady. Yet there was something about this man that intrigued her. Perhaps it was the way his eyes sparkled as he smiled at her, or the way he didn't seem to mind that her hair was a disheveled mess from sleep and her face free of powder. She felt he was seeing the real her, with none of the finery or cosmetics. It was both embarrassing and endearing.

She'd almost forgotten to answer his question.

They sat together on the front step, the cold of the stone permeating her skin through her nightgown as the nearby trees whispered in the wind. His warmth beside her blocked some of the icy breeze.

"It is common in our family," Bizzie replied, crossing her arms in front of her. "To bleed a lot."

"This is what happens every time John scrapes or cuts his skin?" he asked, his eyes widening with surprise. She wanted to ask him his name but felt it would be rude to ignore his questions.

"Tonight is extreme, but yes. His blood doesn't clot like most people's," she replied. For the first time that night, she wondered who or what gave John that cut on his chest. The men hadn't been dressed for hunting; indeed, it was the middle of the night. Had it been a deliberate cut, like her mother had said? Did it happen in that strange room she was never allowed to enter? But the young man asked her a question before she could voice her own.

"You are his sister, correct? Does it happen to you too?"

"Yes, I'm his sister. But no, it doesn't happen to me. It only happens to the men in our family." She craned her neck to glance at the front door, where the sounds of voices and her mother's medicinal work were lost to the night's breeze around them. "Are my brothers and my father all right, or were they wounded tonight too?"

"They're fine," he said, his voice kind. "It is hereditary then? This...condition?"

"My father once told me it's been the curse of families like ours since time *immemorial*," she repeated the word with the same vigor as her father had once said it to her when she was thirteen. "It's even written about in the Talmud. If any descendants of Abraham had two or more sons who died from circumcision, their next son would not."

The man visibly winced at her words. "Your father told you that?"

"Yes," she said, wondering how much longer she'd have to sit in the cold, answering this man's questions. "Why?"

There was a pause. "I must say, seeing how your brother bled tonight from such a small wound, I'm surprised any of the men in your family live long enough to reproduce."

Memories of her mother's healing actions after John or any of her brothers were hurt or fell ill flashed through her memory. Indeed, the four were all lucky to be alive.

She looked out at the night. The full moon

illuminated the lawns and fields surrounding Doneraile Court. Just down the hill, the River Awbeg gurgled around a bend. An owl hooted in the distance. Tree branches rustled in the wind, whispering their secrets. By day, crows caw and spring from the branches, but by night, the sleeping blackbirds blend into the tree's leafless silhouettes.

The door behind Bizzie and her companion opened with a creak, and they were bathed in lantern light. William Simon, the family's butler, appeared wearing the same short white apron as the visiting gentlemen. He looked down on the pair, glancing at Bizzie in poorly concealed alarm before he cleared his throat and said, "Mr. Aldworth? He is awake. We can continue."

Mr. Aldworth, she repeated silently.

Bizzie led Mr. Aldworth back into the house, warmth washing over them as they left the chill of the night behind. Most of the men had disappeared, those remaining murmuring to each other as they headed for the lodge room door.

"What's going on?" she asked the young man, who turned to look at her. He held a strange confidence, regarding her with a look that was neither impolite nor respectful.

"Don't concern yourself, miss," he said. "There

are still a few hours left until sunrise. I suggest you find your bed."

With that, he turned and disappeared behind the closed door, leaving Bizzie in the hallway where her mother stood, looking exhausted with the now-empty bowl and mortar and pestle in her hands.

"Come," she said. "John's fine now. Let's go back to bed."

"What's in that room, Mother? What were they doing in there?"

"Enough, Elizabeth," sighed Lady Doneraile, turning away from her. "Go back to your room."

It was no use arguing. The wind rattled the windowpanes as Bizzie climbed back into her sheets, frustration pummeling her. What was going on in that strange room? Had John willingly let himself be cut? What kind of event took place in the middle of the night that involved stabbing each other? What did those strange things on the oval table mean?

And why was she not allowed to know?

Her last, lingering thought before sleep claimed her was of Mr. Aldworth and his kind, hazel eyes.

Chapter 2

THE LODGE ROOM

October 1712

Bizzie awoke the next morning, her mind racing with questions. Her peek inside the lodge room hadn't cured her curiosity, but instead piqued it further. The glowing candles. The shining metal objects. John's pierced skin.

After dressing in a simple gown of blue, and a half-hearted attempt to fix her hair, Bizzie padded quietly down the hall. She could hear the servants stirring downstairs, but her parents and brothers were all still sleeping after the late night.

She sneaked down the staircase toward the lodge room. She would never ask for permission to enter. *Why ask, she thought, when I know I'll be told no?*

The painted eyes of her ancestors hanging in the hall seemed to follow her as she creeped along. A life-sized portrait of Sir Ralph St. Leger, the Crusader, hung on the wall just beyond the lodge room door, watching her approach but saying nothing.

Her heart was beating with feverish excitement in her breast. She had been kept in the dark long enough. Finally, she would find out the truth. With fingers shaking, she reached out to open the door. Inhaling sharply, she pulled up the metal latch, long tarnished by fingerprints. It didn't budge.

"God's trousers!" she cursed.

Of course, it was locked. But there was another way in.

She glanced over at the door to the library. Inside, the library and the lodge room were connected by an interior door.

Bizzie had always been allowed in the library, of course, though she'd been asked never to venture through the heavy wooden door that led to the secret room. It was always locked anyway; she'd tried once or twice. Would luck allow her access from there today? She'd waited long enough for answers.

The library had always been a haven for Bizzie. She would sit for hours among the bookshelves, reading and imagining the faraway places and people described in the pages of leather-bound books collected by her parents and their parents before them.

The scent of paper and oakwood was a comfort.

The grand windowsills, padded with cushions, were best for watching the comings and goings of visitors to Doneraile Court. She loved when it rained; she'd collect candles and lanterns, turning pages and getting lost in the worlds within while the world outside passed her by.

One of Bizzie's favorite books in their collection was The Faerie Queene, a poem that filled six volumes, all bound in calfskin. The author, Edmund Spenser, had penned it one hundred years before in nearby Kilcolman Castle before it burned to the ground during the Nine Years' War.

A writer in a castle—it all sounded so romantic to Bizzie. She remembered the days when she and her best friend, Rhiannon, would sit for hours in the library, turning the fragile old pages and reading the passages, trying to figure out what the frivolous language meant.

"Him so I sought, and so at last I found," Rhiannon had read aloud, tucking a fiery red curl behind her tanned ear. "Where him that witch had thralled to her will, in chains of lust and lewd desires abound."

They'd both giggled at that.

"See?" said Rhiannon, whispering as her green eyes widened. "Witchcraft."

Bizzie missed her cheerful friend. She smiled remembering her happy times with Rhiannon and the library itself.

No one had been allowed in the library since construction began inside several weeks before. It had been a long, lonely time, where Bizzie had been forced to survive with just one or two books at a time. She disliked reading in her bedroom or the parlor, which were full of distractions.

"If you're caught, just beg for forgiveness," Bizzie muttered to herself as she crept toward the library door. Her family was sleeping, but the servants were returning early from their monthly night off. The scent of cooking wafted from the kitchens on the back side of the house.

Her feet came to a stop just before the library door. She could hear the faint, scratchy sound of a chisel scraping at something on the other side. She gingerly reached for the handle.

"Óró! Ar ais an obair, a bodach!" a man bellowed on the other side of the door just as Bizzie's fingers brushed the handle. "Get back to work, you lazy bum!"

She jumped from the door like it had burnt her. Almost at once, the metallic clanks of two hammers hitting chisels echoed back and forth. She blew a breath from her lips, feeling foolish at her skittishness.

"Just beg for mercy if they catch you," she whispered to herself and lifted the latch.

Seventeen years of growing up as a member of the St. Leger family had taught her it was better to ask for forgiveness than for permission. It had always worked with her father. His blue eyes would soften, and he'd click his tongue in amusement before sending her off to play. It only worked sometimes with her mother, who seemed to know when Bizzie was aware she'd done something wrong and opted to do it anyway. But the person who caught the trespassing young woman that morning was neither of her parents.

"What are you doing?" said a rough voice as a heavy hand landed on her shoulder. Another jolt of fear shot down to her fingertips as she spun around, shaking off the man's hand. She came eye to eye with the butler, William Simon. Sharp eyes, blue like her father's but with none of the warmth, narrowed as he surveyed her, his hand falling from her shoulder.

"I'm getting a book. What else would I be doing?" said Bizzie, lifting her chin and placing her hands on her hips like she'd seen her mother do with her servants.

The middle-aged butler, with one smart step, placed himself between her and the library door. Bizzie didn't know why she felt so nervous. *Calm down! She thought to herself. You haven't done anything wrong…yet.*

"There are no books in there right now, as you know, miss," he said. His words always contained the politeness expected of a butler, but he spoke to them with a cold tone, almost verging on sarcastic. "They're stacked in the parlor. Look there." He gestured to the room on the other side of the main hall, where the books had been shoved in whatever free corner the servants could find.

This won't work. She slid her hands from her hips, softening her stance into one of polite innocence. "William." She tilted her head and gazed up at him. "What's happening in there? Why can't I see?"

He stared her down as she looked back. His skin was lined, crow's feet wrinkles at the corners of his narrowed eyes. He was not quite old, but too much time in the sun made his skin leathery. To Bizzie, he looked like he was hovering on the edge between middle-aged and elderly. He didn't answer her question.

Bizzie's back straightened. "What happened to John last night?"

He must know the answer. Servants saw everything. William had been here the night before. He and the others went to the lodge room in their fancy clothes and strange aprons once a month, always on a night of the full moon.

"It's not any of your concern, Miss Elizabeth," said William finally, his face still and stoic, like a gargoyle's. "Run along now."

Disappointment drilled through her as he shooed her off like a misbehaving child. *I will find out the truth. Somehow!*

Chapter 3

THE HEDGEROW MAZE

October 1712

Early morning mist lingered on the lawn as Bizzie slammed the front door, voicelessly expressing her distaste at William's unsatisfactory answer. She rounded the house, the gray stones dark and foreboding in the meager dawn light. She stayed close to the walls to keep out of the sightlines of nosy servants who might peek out the windows to spy on her.

She headed for the hedgerow maze in the back gardens, holding her skirt to not get it tangled in the bushes, grass whispering against her ankles. The gardens were a full acre of waist-high box hedges planted in a pattern of intricate parallel shapes.

Doneraile Court was built around 1690, a few years before Bizzie was born. It was one of the largest homes in Munster Plantation that wasn't a castle. It was a three-story house of gray stone that had been repurposed from the castle where her father was born and now lay in ruins on the other side of the estate. The castle was surrounded by fields and trees, and Bizzie was told the mighty building could be seen from a half-mile away. Bizzie ran her fingers along the gray stone of Doneraile Court, wondering at the history of the castle that had now served to provide the materials for her home. She liked to imagine the castle had a noble history of knights and kings and dragon-fighting shield-maids, but the reality wasn't as magical as the books in the library.

For English landowning families like the St. Legers who lived in the plantations of Ireland, castles had become unfashionable. They were unpleasant, drafty things, with difficult upkeep, and many people now favored the homier mansions like the one in which Bizzie and her family now dwelled. It was a show of wealth as well as comfort.

Their neighbors, the Jefferys, had decided to build a proper house with brick walls, planked wooden floors, glass windows, and a timber roof rather than live in the fortress of a tower house already built on the land they owned. Blarney Castle was topped with a stone the Gaels claimed was magical, but the ancient castles of Ireland and their stories meant little to New English landowners. Comfort was now de rigueur.

"A pleasant morning to you, Miss Bizzie," said Mick O'Sullivan, barely looking up as he snipped away wayward branches on the hedgerows with the steady, rhythmic crack of his clippers.

"Mick," said Bizzie, not returning the gardener's pleasantries. "Why do we call this a maze when there's no chance of getting lost?"

That gained his attention. Mick turned his sea-green eyes to her, rubbing at the stubble on his chin that was nowadays flecked with more grey than pale brown. "Why, I'm afraid I don't know."

"There's no single starting place, no dead ends, no twists and turns!" she exclaimed, throwing out a hand toward the hedgerows in demonstration. "No final exit, and no sense of accomplishment!"

Mick gave a thoughtful nod at her words as Bizzie regarded the too-straightforward pathways through the garden. Despite the truth to her words, that this was not a real puzzle, she couldn't help but admire the hedges' symmetry.

"How did you get them this way, so perfectly formed?" she asked, folding her arms against the breezy cold of the October morning. "Are those squares exact right angles? What is the circumference of these round ones?"

She was showing off her knowledge, but also

distracting herself from her burning curiosity about the lodge room, asking questions she didn't really care about in order to let go of her frustrations. Mick blinked at her.

"Are these questions not for your father, Miss Bizzie?" he asked. "These are his design, after all. I just keep them tidy," he gave his shears a playful snap. Mick did indeed take marvelous joy at making sure the hedgerows remained perfectly flat on their tops and sides. She said as much, earning a broad smile from the friendly gardener.

Doneraile Court's garden maze rivaled that of Hampton Court's in England, or so she'd heard. Mick seemed eager to keep it that way, and though a part of Bizzie didn't see what the fuss was about, another part of her couldn't help but feel the same way.

She wandered through the hedges, running her fingertips over the tops of the bushes, feeling for loose twigs sticking up higher than they should be.

"Here's one," she called to Mick whenever she felt a poke or a disturbance in the flatness. "There's one here, too."

'Don't you have anything better to do?" grumbled Mick from a few hedges away, armed with his trusty clippers. "I'll fix these imperfections, Lady

Elizabeth. There should still be some raspberries growing over there. Wouldn't you like to pick some?"

Her "help" wasn't wanted. When Mick called her "Lady Elizabeth" it generally meant he was holding onto his rapidly deteriorating patience. He'd called her that when she was small and running amok in the gardens, upsetting the roses.

Bizzie followed the direction of Mick's dirty fingernail to a patch of raspberries along the stone garden wall. To her surprise, there were indeed a few late blooming berries ripe for the picking, rare for this time of year. She picked a handful of the best-looking ones and left without saying goodbye to Mick. As she turned the little pink berries over in her hand, the clinking and clanking of a tinker's cart and the clopping of horse's hooves reached her ears from the other side of the estate wall.

A thrill of excitement tingling through her, she ran to the gate that separated her father's estate from Doneraile's Fishpond Lane and watched the tinker make his way up the cobblestone street, his red and raw chapped hands gripping the reins of a grey mare, sitting on his cart with a ragged top hat on his head.

"Pots and pans! New or used!" he bellowed to

the surrounding houses. His voice was powerful from a career of practice, and his deep voice echoed down the street along with the steady clopping of his horse and the metallic clanking of his cart. "Anything broke? I can fix it! Get your pots and pans here!"

"Tinker!" Bizzie called out to him, waving with her free hand.

"Ah, Miss Bizzie!" the tinker's face broke into a warm grin. "Heard me coming, did you?"

He hopped off his cart and tied his horse to a nearby hitching post.

"What have you got for me today?" she asked, leaning on the locked iron gate that separated them. "Where have your travels taken you?"

There was something romantic about being a traveling worker, not tied down to a single place. The tinker and his wife were not what her mother would say part of "their crowd," but they were a friendly couple and always made time to talk to her. She'd heard they had children of their own, but they were all grown up and had gone their own way.

"Ah, let's see," said the tinker, a sparkle in his eye. "I've been through Buttevant and Mallow, spent some wonderful nights under the stars there. Then onto Newmarket and Kanturk—"

"Tell her about the house in Newmarket!" barked a voice from inside the cart as the tinker's wife appeared. Her mass of curly brown and gray striped hair popped out of the curtain covering the back of the cart, which doubled as their home.

"Why, yes," said the tinker. "Isn't there a fine new house going up there?"

"It's so fine it has two facades. Two!" said his wife, leaping out of the cart and hitting the ground with a thud of threadbare boots. "But one of them isn't real."

Bizzie wasn't sure what she meant by not real, and her eyebrows cocked in confusion. "Why would one need two facades?" she asked the tinker.

"Well, one is good and proper, with steps leading to a door."

"But it's on the side of the house!" his wife bellowed. "Have you ever heard anything like it?"

"Right," said the tinker. "The skinnier side of a rectangle, see?" he made a rectangle with his grubby thumbs and forefingers and Bizzie nodded, understanding.

"On one of the wider sides, which you'd think would be the front of the house, there is…" His brown eyes went blank. "Uh, what do you call it?"

"An alcove," his wife offered matter-of-factly,

clearly proud she knew the answer. She stayed by the cart, petting the mare's neck and cooing softly in her ear.

"Right. An alcove, there," said the tinker, using his chin to point to a wider side of his finger formation. "Like a church," he lowered his voice and neared Bizzie between the bars, who listened in fascination. "Where the statue of a saint would be like."

"It's where a door should be," said his wife, catching the tinker's voice on the wind. "But there isn't one! There isn't even a statue in that alcove. It's empty! Don't you think that's odd, little Bizzie?"

"Very odd," said Bizzie, nodding.

"Odd, indeed," the tinker agreed. "But they bought some bits and bobs of metal from us, so we're happy."

"Here," said Bizzie. She deposited the raspberries into the tinker's outstretched hand. "It's all I have for now. Wild raspberries in October. Isn't that lucky?"

"It is lucky. Thank you," said the tinker, his fingers closing gently over the fruit like they were precious and fragile. He tipped his hat. "Until next time, Miss Bizzie. Any requests?"

"Yes," she said. "Is there a lady of that house in

Newmarket?"

"We'll see, Miss Bizzie!" called the tinker's wife as she clambered back into the cart, ragged skirts swishing behind her. "We shall see!"

Chapter 4

THE LIBRARY

October 1712

When Bizzie pushed open the heavy front door and stepped back inside the quiet splendor of Doneraile Court, her heart leaped. The door to the library was ajar.

"Hello?" she yelled up the stairs, wondering if William was waiting behind some corner, watching. There was no response.

She called down the back hall toward the kitchen. Silence greeted her. Even the chiseling and hammering had ceased. Had everyone left? Was this her chance to glimpse the lodge room at last?

Excitement seized her heart as she glanced back at the polished oak of the library door. She couldn't ignore this chance. She approached it, her footsteps light, and slowly pushed it open with a creak.

The room was almost unrecognizable. The bookshelves were bare, making the place bizarrely look much smaller. The furniture was gone, except for her father's prized pendulum clock. It stood in its usual place in the corner, its shape easy to define beneath the white sheet covering it. Dust mites danced in the daylight, the wooden shelves lonely without the usual weight and color of the books. Although they were still in the house, it was sad to see them gone from their rightful place.

The cushioned window seat looked out to Fishpond Lane, and if you craned your neck right, you could see the river. Bizzie ran her fingers along the plush seat, her reading space since she was small. At least this couldn't be moved.

To her shock, the door leading to the lodge room wasn't closed like it normally was. It wasn't there at all.

Somebody had taken it off its hinges and propped it on its side, between the two windows that overlooked Fishpond Lane. The frame had been dismantled, and a pile of splintered wood lay discarded on the floor. A gaping rectangular hole was there instead. Bizzie would have been able to peer freely into the lodge room had the frame not also been covered by a white sheet.

A pallet of new red bricks was stacked in a neat block nearby, stark and ugly in what was once a place of quiet academia. She approached the pallet and picked up one of the bricks. It was rough to the touch, weighing heavy in her hand.

"Elizabeth!"

The sound of her mother's voice made Bizzie drop the brick. It tumbled from her hand, landing with a thump just missing her right foot.

"It's Bizzie!" she yelled back. She felt foolish. William may have shooed her away before, but she wasn't breaking any rules by being in her own library.

"I can see you're busy, Elizabeth," said Lady Doneraile, chuckling at her own pun as she strolled across the threshold from the hallway. Bizzie's mother had decided to start calling her daughter by her given name earlier that year and had even made an announcement to their family one night during their evening meal, much to the young girl's embarrassment.

"Now that your sister has started her monthly flow," Lady Doneraile had said. She'd overestimated the maturity of her sons, who'd snickered into their food while Bizzie's cheeks had blazed, "We shall all start calling her Elizabeth. She may be married sometime soon, so she deserves a proper lady's name."

Arthur, John, and Hayes had all exploded into laughter.

"A lady! Ha!" John had yelled, throwing the heel of a loaf of bread across the table at Bizzie. She'd caught it and hurled it right back, hitting him square in the forehead.

"Ow!" he'd moaned, exaggerating as he clutched his forehead. "Am I bleeding? I won't stop bleeding if I am, and it'll be all your fault."

"You *shee* that?" Arthur had slurred, pausing to take a long sip from his flask. The family's tenant farmers had taught Arthur how to make *poitin*, a spirit so potent it was illegal across Ireland. Arthur partook more often than Bizzie's mother liked.

"Bizzie is basically a boy, *monthly flow* or not," said Hayes, earning several more snickers from his brothers as their mother sighed. "That's what we've always called her, and you can't stop us from calling her that now. Bizzie Busybody!"

The St. Leger children had each been born a year apart: Arthur, then Hayes, then John, then poor Mary, and lastly, Elizabeth. It was the boys who had coined the nickname Bizzie when they were wee and couldn't pronounce "Elizabeth." Bizzie doubted that any of the young men, now aged nineteen to twenty-one, could pronounce it today if they tried, especially Arthur after a flask of *poitin*.

They'd all ignored her mother's plea and

continued calling their sister by her childhood nickname. But Bizzie couldn't ignore her mother now. Lady Doneraile grabbed her daughter by the wrist.

"I wasn't doing anything!" Bizzie squeaked, trying to wriggle her arm from her mother's grip. Anger rippled through her; she wasn't a child. But it wouldn't do any good to lose her temper here. Instead, she lowered her head. "*Beg for forgiveness, not permission,*" she reminded herself.

"I'm sorry, Mother. I just missed the library. I didn't think it would hurt to look inside."

Behind her mother, Bizzie spotted Arthur and Hayes. John was in bed recuperating from his loss of blood the night before. The other two brothers stood in silence, forming a human barricade in front of the sheet shielding the opening to the lodge room, their eyebrows raised.

"Let's go," said Lady Doneraile, her hand sliding up to Bizzie's shoulder as she pulled her from the library. "Let us leave them to their work."

"Why do they get to stay?" Bizzie asked, frustration bubbling up in her. She'd come so *close* this time.

"They are men, my dear," said her mother as they came to the main hall. "That is how it is.

Remember that Elizabeth. And don't let me catch you in here again until the wall is built."

Bizzie glared at her brother Arthur, who winked at her as their mother closed the door behind them.

Chapter 5

RHIANNON

February 1711

Bizzie St. Leger and Rhiannon Simon had been best friends since the day Rhiannon and her father, William, first knocked on the door of Doneraile Court the year before.

Usually, Mr. Casserly opened the door to guests, but the butler had just recently died in an accident which Lord and Lady Doneraile told everyone it was best not to speak about.

Lady Doneraile was sitting knitting in the nearby parlor when the strong knock came at the front door. Not expecting any visitors that day, Lady Doneraile had taken it upon herself to answer the door instead of waiting for one of the servants to come. Bizzie stood at the foot of the stairs behind her, burning with curiosity.

"Yes? Can I help you?"

"Good afternoon, m'lady," said a well-dressed man about Lady Doneraile's age. There was a young woman half-hiding behind him. She had fiery-red hair and was wearing a simple gown of green. Both had sun-kissed skin. Their clothes were not dirty but rumpled as though they'd been traveling. The man's ice-blue eyes were stark against his dark face.

"I understand you just lost your butler. God rest his poor soul. My name is William Simon, and I'm here to apply for the position."

"Yes. Mr. Casserly," Lady Doneraile pushed the memory of his waterlogged body from the front of her mind. "It was a most unfortunate tragedy," she said tilting her head to eye the girl behind William. "And who might this be? Your daughter?"

"Yes, m'lady, this is Rhiannon." He nudged the girl, who gave a tiny shy curtsy before hiding behind him again. "But I promise she won't get in the way. She's a good lass, works hard."

Bizzie saw her mother's shoulders tense as her eyes fell on the young girl. She looked to be a wee bit older than Bizzie, the same age Mary would have been now. The girl also had Mary's same red locks, a feature that Bizzie's brother Hayes shared. As Bizzie clutched the stairs' polished wooden newel post, something stirred in her too.

Bizzie had only been six at the time, and though she didn't remember much of the incident herself, she had heard the servants talk about it so many times she sometimes felt she'd seen it all with her own youthful eyes. Young Mary, only in her seventh summer, had been warned about the dangers of the berries that grew in the yew tree, but she hadn't been able to resist them. She had been the rebellious type, once burning her hand on the fire grate mere moments after her mother had asked her not to touch it.

She had been wandering the gardens when her eyes had fallen on several of the brightly colored berries at the foot of a yew tree, freshly fallen and not yet picked by birds or trampled underfoot. The little girl had picked up a handful and hidden in a bush in the garden, giggling at her victory as she'd shoved them into her mouth.

It had only taken several moments for Mary's mirth to turn to horror. She'd turned weak and cold, her whole body trembling as she threw up, her skin pasty-white and a cold sweat across her skin. Mick O'Sullivan had found her lying in the grass, her skin pale as snow and her breathing labored.

"Lord Doneraile, sir!" he'd screamed in a panic, gathering the child in his arms and running inside. "Lady Doneraile! Mary is sick!"

He'd run to fetch a doctor while Lady Doneraile

had scrambled to prepare a concoction of ipecacuanha root, in a desperate attempt to make the girl vomit. The servants were bringing buckets of water and wet cloths. But it was too late; Mary collapsed and never got up again. The doctor had examined her with a grim face, confirming what everybody feared with solemn, short words that made Lady Doneraile wail and sob, the terrible sound of a mourning mother that would haunt the family and servants' dreams for years. The whole incident had shaken the family to its very core.

After the funeral, Lady Doneraile had taken a personal revenge on yew trees, demanding that every yew tree on the Doneraile estate be chopped down and burned. But the poisonous seeds inside the berries refused to die as easily as they had killed her young daughter. Despite her best efforts, and those of Mick and several other gardeners, new yew trees popped up every spring, as though mocking the grieving mother.

In fact, Mick O'Sullivan was ripping one of the beastly things out of the pasture just over the man's shoulder as Lady Doneraile and William Simon spoke.

"M'lady?" he said nervously, eyeing her blank expression.

42

"Yes. I'm sorry," she said, her voice soft. "She just…reminds me of someone I once knew."

"Please, m'lady," said William Simon. "Her mother died during our journey on the ship here. We have nowhere else to go, and I have worked as a butler before. We shan't disappoint you."

Bizzie's heart went out to the pair as the redheaded girl looked down, her fiery locks hiding her face.

Lord Doneraile appeared in the front hall, glancing over his wife's shoulder. "Who is this?"

"Simon, sir. William Simon," said the man, extending a hand. Lord Doneraile's eyes narrowed in suspicion, but his expression relaxed when he took the man's hand and gave it a firm shake, his fingers wrapping around William Simon's wrist. Then they stepped toward one another, foot to foot, knee to knee. They embraced like old friends, chest to chest, and patted each other on the backs. William Simon whispered something into Lord Doneraile's ear, and a smile spread on the lord's face. Their strange ritual complete, Bizzie's father said, "Come, we have lodging by the garden maze where you should be comfortable."

As Lord Doneraile settled William Simon into a small cottage by the hedgerows, Bizzie shyly approached the new butler's daughter. They were close in age, though Rhiannon was taller and as wild-looking as the adventurous maidens in her favorite books.

"Hello," she said, giving a polite curtsy. "I'm Elizabeth, but you can call me Bizzie. Everyone does."

"Good morning, miss," said the girl, returning the curtsy. "I'm Rhiannon Simon. You can call me Rhiannon."

They both giggled. "Would you like me to show you around?" Bizzie liked the look of the girl. She seemed shy and sweet, and Bizzie didn't have many people to spend time with other than her brothers. The only other girl near their age was Brigid, the Casserlys' daughter and she had already gone off and married one of the local farmers.

"Do you like to read? I can show you the library later. It's just marvelous." She wondered whether the girl could read at all, but Rhiannon gave an eager nod. Bizzie knew redheaded people to be pale and often freckled, like her brother Hayes, but Rhiannon's skin was darker, like it had been warmed by the sun.

"Why is your skin so brown?" she asked bluntly.

The girl blushed. "I grew up in Barbados," she

explained, looking politely around the hedgerows, her hands clasped together. "It's an island in the West Indies where winter never comes. They call us 'redlegs' though. Because of the sunburns we get," she added when Bizzie gave a puzzled frown.

Bizzie tried to imagine a world without the cold sheets of rain and the snow that fell in the chillier months, but she couldn't quite manage it. "How is it then that you look and sound just like us if you were born in the new world?"

"I am just like you," said Rhiannon, reaching to wrap a red curl around her finger. "My whole family is. We were sent there from here. We didn't have a choice."

"What do you mean?"

"Ah, you know nothing, do you, Bizzie St. Leger?" said the girl, suddenly sounding very grown-up. Bizzie stared at her for a moment, then she burst out laughing.

"I do know some things!" she said, giving the girl a playful push. "But I don't know why you and your family were sent to Barbados. Tell me."

"We were once like you and lived here in Ireland," said the girl, who Bizzie liked more with every passing moment. "But we were "Barbadozed," as they call it."

"Bar-Barbadozed?"

"My family refused to accept Oliver Cromwell as our lord protector." Bizzie recognized the name as one seldom spoken, even more than six decades after he conquered Ireland. Rhiannon picked at a hangnail, not looking at Bizzie. "They...they stripped us of all our land and belongings and sent us onto ships to Barbados to work. Like slaves."

Horror rippled through Bizzie. She couldn't imagine losing everything—their house, their land, all their lovely servants—then being sent off to a strange land and being forced to work in the burning sun miles from home across the sea. Sympathy battled awkwardness as the girl fiddled with her hands. She didn't know what to say.

"It's hard to believe there was ever a time when England didn't have a king or queen," said Bizzie eventually, at a loss of what else to offer. "I can't even imagine it."

"Well, neither could my great-grandfather," said Rhiannon. They continued walking, the gentle breeze blowing the grass against their ankles, heading back toward the great mansion where Bizzie would show Rhiannon the library and the ground floor.

"He was rounded up by Cromwell's men and

sent on a ship to Barbados. His servitude was only supposed to last ten years. But it didn't matter. My grandfather was born in Barbados. My father too. He met and married my mother there, and only recently were we set free and allowed to come home." She inhaled, as though smelling the cold Irish air. "I heard so many stories from my family of Ireland, of how wonderful it was. It's good to finally be here, to see it with my own eyes. I may have been born in Barbados, but this is my home. I can feel it."

After a quick tour of the hedgerows, where Rhiannon delighted at the delicate symmetry of the hedgerows, and the bare raspberry bushes where Bizzie promised they'd pick fruit together next season, they headed inside to the library.

Rhiannon gasped in delight at the collection of books, more than they could ever hope to read in a lifetime. The girls found a quiet corner among the shelves and with sunlight pouring in the window. Bizzie was excited. She had a new friend, and there was a certain thrill about talking quietly among the books, like they had secrets to hide.

"What was the ship from Barbados like?" Bizzie whispered, imagining unfurling sails, shouting sailors, and a salty sea breeze. It made her heart quicken with excitement. She had read stories about ships, of course, but how thrilling it would be to experience it for real!

"It was - " Rhiannon paused. "My mother got sick on the journey." Her voice cracked as her eyes, glassy with tears, looked to the ceiling as though searching for refuge from her pain. "She didn't survive. We had to bury her at sea."

It was a sad tale.

"She deserved better," said Bizzie softly, and she hugged the girl, the sunlight shining in their hair. When she withdrew, a tear slipped down Rhiannon's tanned cheek.

"You're safe now," she found herself saying. "My father seems to like your father. I think he'll give him a job. Everything will be all right, you'll see."

It didn't take long for the girls to become fast friends despite the vast differences in their upbringing. When William Simon was officially welcomed into Lord Doneraile's employ as their new butler, the girls went on picnics together, read books by candlelight, and told each other secrets. They confessed which young men in town they liked, giggling and teasing each other.

"Don't you think the baker's son is handsome?"

Rhiannon whispered one day as they wandered through Doneraile, baskets full of flowers and fresh bread.

Bizzie scrunched up her nose. "He speaks improperly and is missing teeth."

"Hmm, you're right. Maybe if he doesn't talk…"

They fell into peals of giggles, earning sharp looks from passers-by.

They also swapped tales of their adventures. Bizzie felt her life in Doneraile Court was rather boring compared to the wonder of the far-off Barbados, where summer never ended, and white-sand beaches stretched for miles; however, she came up with some stories of her own.

She told Rhiannon all about the ghost at the nearby Castle Pook who collected and washed people's clothes, returning them pressed and folded. Rhiannon gave a loud laugh that made several nearby birds flap away in alarm. She threw her head back as she clutched her chest.

"Oh, I can think of worse things a ghost could do!" she chuckled. "A laundry-loving ghost, who would have thought! Back in Barbados, there are witches who will teach you love spells for a price. Let's try one out!" she suddenly said, clutching Bizzie's wrist as her green eyes shone. "You could use the help. Your mother wants you to start courting, right?"

"I don't know," said Bizzie slowly, sliding her arm from Rhiannon's grip. "I mean, it sounds…" Her voice trailed off, not quite knowing how to say it. She finally settled on 'strange.'

Bizzie wasn't much interested in marriage yet, but if it did happen for her, she wanted it to be on her own terms. Would a magic spell really work, or was it superstitious nonsense from a people half a world away?

Rhiannon giggled. "If nothing happens, then no harm done," she said. "Come on, I'll race you up the hill."

Chapter 6

UNSUITABLE

August 1711

Now that Bizzie was nearing womanhood, her mother was encouraging her to start courting and find a good suitor she would eventually marry. It was the same for all high-society girls, and though she didn't feel particularly ready to marry, it was a rite of passage she'd embrace with all the grace she could.

Her latest attempted match was with a young suitor named Arundel Hill, the son of one of their neighbors. It had started strong, or so she'd thought. Pink-cheeked and short of stature, sporting a small goatee he was strangely proud of—he stroked it often around his chin as if he was in deep thought but wasn't. One day Arundel had come to call on her one day with a gift. It was a long-toothed comb topped with an intricate silver filigree design of entangled flowers and leaves. Bizzie didn't care much for hair accessories, but she supposed it was pretty and it was thoughtful of the young man to give it to her.

"To keep your hair in place," Arundel had said, casting a glance at the wilder auburn strands that had a habit of coming loose from the knot at the top of her head. Her mother had insisted she wear a dress and do her hair for the meeting, but Bizzie's auburn locks always seemed to have a mind of their own. It amused her that Arundel might hope to tame it with a simple comb.

She was more interested in finding out what Arundel knew of his father's tenants. There was a lot she could learn from him, and she'd heard some unfavorable rumors about the way he and his family treated them. After all, an easy way to see a man's true nature was to see how they treated their subordinates. How would he treat her as his wife?

"Do tell me, Arundel," she purred as he came in at her invitation, removing his hat and looking respectfully around the foyer as though he had never stepped foot inside Doneraile Court before. 'What are your family's tenants' houses like? What kinds of things do they like to eat? What are their names?"

Arundel looked crestfallen at her greater interest in his tenants than him, and after stumbling through several pressing questions, he excused himself early with a mumble of, "I hope you enjoy the comb, Miss Elizabeth."

He bumped into Bizzie's father on his way out, and she heard him say, "She isn't ready to marry, Lord Doneraile. She still seems far too young."

Bizzie stopped at the staircase, torn between wanting to see her father's reaction and longing to escape to the sanctuary of her bedroom.

Lord Doneraile thanked him for coming. He squeezed the shorter man's shoulder and said, "I will see you here at the next full moon."

Arundel pulled on his hat, gave it a polite tip, and left in a swirl of suit jacket tails.

Bizzie's interaction with James Coppinger, her next hopeful suitor, went even more poorly, and it was a memory that still left her indignant and more than a little confused. The Irish ladies of the house were quick to deliver their opinion as to why it had taken such a turn for the unfortunate. Bizzie heard their exchange when she was sneaking to the pantry for a bit of bread, just days after her visit with James.

"Isn't it because of her endless questions?" asked Mrs. Casserly, the head housekeeper.

"Or because we had to let her gown's waistline out again?" asked Mrs. Cunnane, the cook. Bizzie could imagine the older lady shaking her head.

She listened, self-consciously patting her stomach, knowing what they said might be true, but none of them hit the right reason for her apparent failure.

Bizzie had known James Coppinger since they were wee. He had grown up less than a mile from Doneraile Court, and they had shared many adventures with her brothers climbing, running through the hedgerow mazes, and hiding in the bushes to spy on passing travelers. Most of their reunion had been reminiscing their younger days, when their friendship had been simple and innocent.

"Do you remember when you fell into the river that time, dress and all?" the young man had laughed, warm eyes crinkling at the memory. She'd supposed he was handsome; his boyish features had matured to that of a young man's, with high cheekbones and strong shoulders. He didn't make her heart flutter like in the books she'd read. Perhaps that feeling only happened in fiction.

"That was funny until John jumped in after me and caught his leg on your fishing hook," she'd remarked. Her brother still had the scar just above his ankle.

His face fell as he winced. "Oh, yes. That was

a bad one. Your mother is a miracle worker with that medicine she makes. I thought the bleeding would never stop." He gave a delicate shudder at the memory of John's profusely bleeding leg.

When they were children, the curse of the never-ending bleeding had landed them in a few close calls. John's skin had been ghost-white that day from blood loss, and it had taken days for the blood on the grass to wash away in the rain.

"But it did." Bizzie grinned. "He's fine, and he's still around to annoy me."

"Oh, you are terrible, Bizzie," James laughed, giving her hand a light slap.

On James' third meeting with Bizzie that week, where they were sitting in the parlor with a pot of tea and talking about the games they used to play in the nearby woods, Rhiannon appeared behind James, a fraction closer than strangers would normally stand. Bizzie could smell the perfume she'd made from crushed berries, and her eyebrows cocked as she regarded her friend. Rhiannon was wearing her best dress and several flowers pinned in her hair.

"What's going on here?" the redheaded girl asked, a smile on her face that said she had a delicious secret. "You're having entirely too much fun, I'm sure. Who is this, Bizzie?"

"Oh, Rhiannon, meet James Coppinger," Bizzie said. On her way to Bizzie's side, Rhiannon let her body brush past the young man with a bit too much familiarity.

"He grew up next door, at Castle Saffron. James, this is my friend Rhiannon. She and her father just moved here from Barbados. Her father is William Simon, the butler."

"How do you do?" said James, kissing Rhiannon's knuckles. She smiled at him, straightening her skirt as she took a seat on a nearby pouf.

It was all over. As soon as James laid eyes on Rhiannon's sun-kissed skin and emerald eyes, Bizzie may as well have been a piece of furniture. All his attention went to Rhiannon, his eyes barely moving from her face as he asked her a thousand questions about herself, from her life in Barbados to her favorite kind of food. Bizzie sat with her rapidly cooling tea, struck by the absurdity of it all.

After a while, she'd grown bored and fetched a book from the library. When she returned to the lounge, neither of them seemed to notice she was ever missing.

"What did you do?" Bizzie whispered to Rhiannon after James left an hour and a half later. He had tripped over himself on the way out, promising

Rhiannon he'd come calling again, tipping his hat. He barely waved goodbye to Bizzie.

The redheaded girl grinned, twirling a strand of her hair in her finger.

"Remarkable, truly," she said aloud. "It looks like it worked."

Impatience ran through Bizzie at her friend's coyness, and she fought to keep her voice level.

"What are you talking about, Rhiannon? What worked?"

"The spell." Her green eyes glittered as she turned to smile at Bizzie. Rhiannon was blushing.

"I put a strand of my hair into the heart-shaped locket built into my mother's wedding ring," Rhiannon explained.

"I took the ring off my mother's hand when she died. It was made by an Irishman in the West Indies decades ago, and it's been in my family ever since. There are others like it, and some have been used for love spells." Bizzie listened to her friend, enchanted but skeptical.

"If you put a tiny lock of your hair in the locket on the ring," Rhiannon continued, "and give it to someone, they will fall in love with you. As I passed your friend James, I dropped it into his pocket. It was easy! And clearly, it worked. Far better than I expected, too."

"But it's not real," Bizzie grumbled. It had stung her that James' attention had instantly dropped as soon as Rhiannon had appeared, spell or no spell. "Why would you want love if it's not true and just a trick?"

Part of her admired Rhiannon's wild way of trying for love; another part of her was indignant. James had come over to spend time with Bizzie, perhaps hopeful of a future together. He'd left utterly enthralled by the butler's daughter instead, casting Bizzie aside without a thought.

"Oh, Bizzie, you don't understand, do you?" sighed Rhiannon.

"Then help me understand." Bizzie's voice was like ice.

"You are the daughter of a lord," she said, taking her friend's hands. Bizzie resisted the urge to pull away from her. "I'm the motherless daughter of a butler. You'll have plenty of options—Arundel Hill already tried, and there's likely a long line of suitors waiting for their chance to court you. This is the best I could hope for." She smiled. "Besides, you didn't really want to marry James Coppinger, did you?"

I'd have liked the option, Bizzie thought to

herself. Because now she didn't have a choice. James went straight home that day to declare that he had his heart set on marrying the girl from Doneraile Court—no, not the eligible Elizabeth St. Leger, daughter of Lord Doneraile, but the daughter of the mansion's butler, Rhiannon Simon.

Bizzie caught wind of some rumors from whispering servants that James' father had greatly opposed the match, appalled that he'd chosen a "half-wild servant girl" over Lord Doneraile's only living daughter.

William Simon, the butler, was of course delighted at the arrangement and boasted about the match to anyone who would listen. Perhaps it was James unmoving and relentless insisting, or his kind-hearted mother's convincing, but his father finally caved, and the pair were married just a few weeks later.

It had passed by like a summer rainstorm, leaving Bizzie drenched in shock.

The wedding took place at Castle Saffron. Rhiannon looked radiant in a gown of white, matching flowers in her red locks, and James had welcomed Bizzie warmly and thanked her for coming. It was the first the pair had talked since he'd fallen under Rhiannon's spell—quite literally—but

Bizzie pushed away her annoyance and greeted him with grace.

Her friend had been right after all. She hadn't had her heart set on marrying James. He was a fond childhood friend, but he didn't make her heart sing like the romantic poems and stories in her favorite library books. Perhaps there was still someone out there for Bizzie who could make her feel this way. In the meantime, she'd put aside her own indignation and be happy for them both.

"This place smells of mold," Bizzie remarked to the bride when they found a quiet corner of the castle to talk. Rhiannon had planted flowers and thistles in every nook and cranny of the otherwise gloomy grey walls, making the place look a little less bleak. Even so, the old castle was an example of why so many residents, Bizzie's family included, had opted for the grand comfort of modern mansions instead of these drafty stone buildings. A positive outcome of Bizzie not marrying James.

"It will do," her friend replied, a fond smile on her face.

Seeing the happiness Rhiannon was feeling, the clenched fist on Bizzie's heart opened, and she did not pause as she slipped her arm through the crook of Rhiannon's elbow. "Even though you stole my suitor, I've forgiven you," she said, and Rhiannon blushed in delight and hugged her. "I'm not sure I forgive him for stealing you though," she mumbled into her shoulder. She would miss her best friend.

Rhiannon would be moving to the other side of the estate walls, and Bizzie was not allowed to cross the boundary unattended. No more picnics or fruit picking, no more walks along the river, no more sneaking treats from the kitchens and sharing a book by candlelight when they couldn't sleep.

"This is for you," Rhiannon said later when the ceremony was over, and a simple wedding band adorned her finger. She presented Bizzie with a wooden box. "No, don't open it here!" she hissed, glancing over Bizzie's shoulder as the girl attempted to pry it open. "Come over here."

They found a shadowy alcove, where Bizzie balanced the box in one hand, carefully opening it with the other. Inside was a piece of slate and some chalk, and beside that was a torn piece of paper with a series of symbols on it. Each symbol represented a letter of the alphabet.

"My father taught this to me in Barbados," she whispered. "When my mother and I were sent to work for another plantation owner. We used this to leave each other messages no one else could read.

Memorize the symbols and then burn the paper. Write me a message on the slate using the code and bury the box under some rocks and leaves in the nook of that Spanish chestnut we found. You know the one down by the river?"

Bizzie nodded. Emotion welled up inside her. This really was goodbye. Her friend looked more mature somehow now that she was Mrs. James Coppinger. Bizzie felt she was being left behind in the dregs of childhood. She clutched the wooden box to her chest, lips pressed together.

"I'll go there when I can and read your message," Rhiannon whispered. "Then leave you one in return."

The girls hugged again, Bizzie's heart a tangle of love, friendship, and bitterness. "I'll write to you," she whispered. "Never forget me, Rhiannon Coppinger."

Chapter 7

The Length of a Cable Tow

October 1712

It had been a few days since John's brush with death and Lord Doneraile had barely let his boy out of his sight since. He had already lost one child and now nearly lost another due to his own negligence and willful arrogance. John did not know what was coming that night, but his father did, and he let it happen, disregarding his son's known condition.

He admitted to himself his actions were unforgiveable, but assured John's health was improving. Lord Doneraile felt safe leaving the house to attend to business, especially now that his wife was speaking to him again.

Sitting in his open carriage, Lord Doneraile listened to the familiar sounds of clopping hooves. He didn't much enjoy traveling house to house to collect rent from his tenant farmers, but taxes to Queen Anne over in England had to be paid.

William Simon was driving, not that the butler said much beyond mild small talk, but that was the way Lord Doneraile liked it. The drive was peaceful when he could ponder, and he was sure William had better things to think about than how to engage his master in trivial topics such as the weather.

They passed over a particularly large bump in the road, making the carriage lurch forward. A strange little squeak sounded beneath Lord Doneraile's seat. Frowning, he lifted the bench cushion to find his daughter curled up in a fetal position, her dress rumpled, his eyebrows rising in surprise. She looked guiltily up at him with her large blue eyes. She may be seventeen now, a woman, but to him, she still looked a child at times. His heart softened.

"I'm sorry, Father," she said meekly, remembering to seek forgiveness. "I just need to see something beyond the walls of Doneraile eCourt very once in a while."

Despite himself, Lord Doneraile chuckled at her mischief. She reminded him of himself when he was young. "I understand," he said, taking pity on her as he helped her out of her cramped hiding space. "Well, you won't see much from in there, will you? Sit with me for a while."

She clambered out in a swirl of skirts and plopped down beside him, hastily straightening the wild auburn locks that had pulled free of her ribbon and rubbing the spot where she'd hit her head. A small lump was growing. It smarted, but she ignored it.

Bizzie was relieved when she realized she wasn't in trouble. Seeing her father's surprise when he caught her in her hiding place made her brace for the back of his hand. Instead, she settled beside him like when she was small, listening to him talk about the surrounding homes with happiness in her heart. Her shoulders relaxed and she gave him a shy smile.

"You see that house over there?" He pointed to a modest home made of stone that sat on a hill, grey smoke puffing lazily from its chimney. "That's the Kelly family residence. They've been keeping sheep here for decades."

As he spoke, their carriage rumbled past fieldstone wall surrounding a herd of sheep, their coats fluffy as they munched on grass and bleated to one another. A ram with a particularly deep voice baaed at them on their way past, making Bizzie giggle.

They stopped for tea at the farm of Mr. and Mrs. O'Donnell, who had their rent and tax money ready. Bizzie enjoyed sitting beside their open window with a cracked mug of steaming tea, looking around at the mud and overgrowing grass, the sounds of snorting pigs and clucking hens coming from the outbuildings and smelling the faint scent of manure. It was a far cry from what she was used to at Doneraile Court.

At the millinery, Mr. Murphy, a squat older man with a permanent worry crease in his forehead, bartered his payments in exchange for a new hat for Lady Doneraile. In a good mood, Lord Doneraile accepted a partial payment, letting Bizzie try on the hat before they went on their way to the next home.

All was going well, Bizzie and her father chattered happily, reveling in their rare time spent alone together. However, Lord Doneraile stopped abruptly, halfway through his sentence, when he spotted a man staggering out of the tavern at the Inn of the Sorrel Horse, on Doneraile Town's main street.

"Stop here," he said, tugging on William's coattails.

"Who's that, Father?" asked Bizzie.

"It's Edmund Synan." The mirth had disappeared from her father's face, his eyes narrowed as he fixed his gaze on the drunkard.

Edmund Synan's family had once lived on the land the St. Legers now owned. Bizzie remembered a story the traveling tinker once told her during one of his trips to town.

"Your families used to be great friends. That is until Cromwell came to Ireland," the tinker had said. "There were two Synan brothers at the time. When Cromwell's cronies asked them if they supported the Lord Protector and rejected the monarchy, the older brother flipped his lid! Started spewing something about rejecting them both, said he was holding out for a 'New World Order' or something like that, with 'liberty and justice for all.' He called it the New Jerusalem. Or was it the New Atlantis?"

Bizzie had listened in fascination, and though a dozen questions jumped to her mind, she listened without interrupting the man. His wife had stood beside him, arms folded as she'd bobbed her head to his words.

"The younger brother saw his chance to usurp his older sibling's inheritance and told Cromwell's cronies he didn't know what his brother was talking about," the tinker went on. "So, they rounded up the older brother, his wife, and his children, and shipped them off overseas somewhere for his defiance."

Just like Rhiannon's family, Bizzie thought.

"Maybe he fell overboard and found old Atlantis.

Who knows?" he gave a chuckle. "I don't know. Regardless, the younger brother thought he'd be getting the land, but ended up with a measly three hundred pounds from your family. It was barely enough to buy the inn. Now that's all they've got, and it looks like Edmund drinks most of it."

Edmund's brown hair was matted and untidy, eyes bleary and reddened from drink. Lord Doneraile climbed out of the carriage with the fluid grace of a gentleman, adjusting his jacket. Bizzie got up to follow him.

"Stay here," he ordered her. Bizzie slumped back in her seat.

William turned to look down at her, his face stern as always. For a moment, Bizzie wondered if he was about to berate her for stowing away in his carriage, privately thinking he was hardly in the position to scold her when her father had not. Instead, the butler grunted something about relieving himself and slid from the carriage to a thicket of trees a little way away.

Bizzie watched as her father tapped the drunken man on the shoulder. Startled, Edmund spun round and blinked stupidly at him until recognition made his face contort in fury.

"You!" he slurred, pointing a finger in Lord

Doneraile's face. He gave her father a hard shove, knocking him to the ground and making Bizzie gasp in shock. Edmund pounced on Lord Doneraile, and knelt on him, using his knees to pin Lord Doneraile's arms to the ground. Bizzie watched in horror, her knuckles whitening as she gripped the carriage door. Should she aid him? Call out for help?

The drunk man raised his hand to slap Lord Doneraile in the face, a well-known sign of a challenge to a duel. Bizzie squeezed her eyes shut and braced for the sound.

The slap never came.

When she opened her eyes, she saw Mr. Aldworth, the kind man with the hazel eyes she'd met just a couple nights before during her father's last meeting in the lodge room. Mr. Aldworth grabbed Edmund by the back of the shirt and tossed him aside. He landed in a clumsy sprawl as her father blinked in surprise.

"Richard, thank you," he managed to sputter out.

Richard, Bizzie silently repeated.

"Get out of here," Mr. Aldworth growled at Edmund. "Now!"

Edmund got drunkenly to his feet, threw them both a look of hatred, and stumbled up the stone steps back into the inn. It took him two bumbling attempts, almost slipping back down to the ground, before he finally shouldered his way inside and slammed the door closed.

"How much does he owe you?" asked Mr. Aldworth, extending a hand to help Lord Doneraile to his feet. Her father said something in a low voice she couldn't hear. There was a series metallic clinks, the sound of coins moving in a bag, and Mr. Aldworth handed a small pouch to her father.

"Thank you, my friend. I'll see you at Doneraile Court the night of the next full moon," Lord Doneraile said, shaking the man's hand and brushing himself off. Straw fluttered to the dirt ground. "If you're not farther away than the length of your cable tow."

Bizzie didn't understand what that meant but it was apparently a joke because Mr. Aldworth laughed. To Bizzie his laugh was a sound full of sunshine. He glanced over Lord Doneraile's shoulder and caught her looking. Smiling, his warm eyes crinkled as he tipped his hat at her. Heat flushing up her neck, Bizzie gave a little wave, watching as he walked away.

Lord Doneraile climbed back into the carriage in silence, looking remarkably composed for a man who'd just been shoved onto his back by a drunkard and nearly challenged to a duel. William reappeared a moment later, and neither Bizzie nor her father said a word to him. The butler didn't seem to have noticed what had just happened.

Lord Doneraile untied the thin gold rope around the dark red pouch and poured several shining coins into his hand, slipping them into his jacket pocket. As the coach rolled into motion, Bizzie's father clutched the empty velvet purse in his hand, not looking at her. The sounds of rickety wooden wheels and clopping horse hooves fell into a rhythmic motion.

"Not a word of this to your mother, Bizzie," he said finally, still staring at the little bag.

"Yes, Father," she hesitated. "I wonder if I might have that?"

He finally looked at her, his eyebrow cocked. He handed it to her, and she grabbed it. This was Richard Aldworth's. Her heart fluttered in her chest when she remembered how he'd looked at her. She found herself smiling as she held the pouch in her fingers.

As the carriage rumbled along the dirt path, passing more grasslands, fields of animals and trees, her father finally broke his silence.

"Bizzie, do you know the story of the great King Solomon?"

"Yes, of course!" she said, quickly stowing the pouch away, eager to prove her knowledge to her father. "There were two women and each of them had a baby and one of the babies died and both women said the living baby was theirs and so King Solomon ordered for it to be cut in half—"

"No, Bizzie," he said, his voice gentle. "I'm thinking of another one, but it's similar. It's about King Solomon's son."

She focused on her father, though she felt a longing to look out at the trees and the hills. A cold breeze blew in from the north, making her shiver. She scooted closer to her father and listened.

"His son had many, many friends," her father said. "King Solomon was concerned, however, that they were not his true friends. He thought perhaps these boys only spent time with him because he was the son of a king. So, he asked his son to invite his best friend to breakfast one day.

"The son had his supposed 'best friend' over the next morning. The boys were served three eggs, and they each ate one. They both insisted the other have the third. After going back and forth, the friend ate it, and King Solomon took offense at this."

"Why?" asked Bizzie, puzzled. "Perhaps his son was just being a gracious host?"

"Perhaps," said Lord Doneraile. "But the same thing happened the next morning with a different friend. Two boys, three eggs. Solomon's son had one, and the other boy had two."

"Well, were they boiled, scrambled, or fried?" Bizzie asked. "A scrambled egg could be shared, while a poached or fried egg, well...that's more difficult, especially if it has a runny yolk."

"They were fried," said her father, his lip twitching in amusement.

"I think I would give my extra egg to my friend," said Bizzie, thinking of Rhiannon. "Especially if my friend usually had less than I did. I'm guessing the king's son could have as many eggs as he wanted, whenever he wanted."

"That's true," said Lord Doneraile. "Would you like to know what happened when King Solomon's son invited another friend over?"

Bizzie leaned into the soft coach seat, enjoying the soothing cadence of her father's voice.

"Solomon's son had a hard time choosing a third friend to have over for breakfast. He finally settled on a boy who was least like his other friends. The son of a peasant."

"Then surely he would get the third egg," Bizzie babbled.

"You'd think so," Lord Doneraile agreed. "But when the servant came with the third egg, the young boy insisted that Solomon's son should have it."

"That's only polite," said Bizzie.

"And, as always, Solomon's son insisted that his guest have the third egg. They argued back and forth for some time while King Solomon watched. It went on so long that the egg grew cold, and they could have had a third or fourth egg each by then. That's when the peasant boy made a suggestion."

"What did he say?"

"He asked the servant for a slice of bread," said Lord Doneraile. "He put the fried egg on top of the bread and sliced both down the middle. The yolk split, of course, which is always the concern, but the bread soaked up the yolk equally. In the end, the boys shared the fried egg and were both happy. And that was how King Solomon knew his son had found a true friend."

Now Bizzie was the one to sit in silence, brooding on the story while her hand snaked into the pocket of her dress. Her thumb stroked the velvet pouch of the stranger who'd just paid another stranger's bills.

Chapter 8

A SLIPPED STITCH

October 1712

When Bizzie and her father arrived home, she found Lady Doneraile knitting in the parlor. The furnished room with sunlight shining through the large windows was warm and rich compared to the starkness of the library across the hall, with its empty bookshelves and ugly pile of bricks.

Hand-carved chairs and upholstered sofas were neatly arranged in the center of the room, their horsehair fabrics dyed to match the charming blues and red in the ornate Persian carpet beneath them. Gold-framed portraits of more English ancestors frowned down from the walls around them. When she was a child, Bizzie feared the intricate oil paintings, feeling like they were watching her. Sometimes she still thought so.

Bizzie took a seat near the fireplace, listening to the comforting crackle and pops as heat washed over her. Her mother handed her a ball of white yarn and two pairs of knitting needles.

"Socks," she explained. "For Brigid's baby. I'll knit one, and you knit the other."

Brigid was the daughter of Lady Doneraile's childhood housemaid who had come along with her to Doneraile Court upon her marriage. Despite being employer and employee, she and Mrs. Casserly were more like sisters.

Lady Doneraile lit a new candle between them, a comforting glow to accompany the light shining through the windows. As the pair worked in contented silence, needles clacking and the fireplace flickering, Bizzie thought about Richard Aldworth. He had been rather dashing when he helped her father today. She imagined him as a strong hero saving her helpless father from the clutches of evil. Never mind it had been a minor spat with a man who had been at the whiskey.

She felt her cheeks burning and was glad of the dim light. Was Bizzie in love? Butterflies took wing in her stomach as she remembered how the well-dressed young man had smiled at her today before striding off on his long legs in a billow of his cloak. How friendly he'd been to her the night of John's injury.

Do I want to see him again? she thought to herself. *Yes, I think I do.*

A sudden loud bang shook the floorboards and startled her and her mother.

"Ow!" Hayes yelled, his deep voice echoing. "That was my foot!"

"Sorry," Arthur replied, though Bizzie caught the tone of amusement in her brother's voice.

Bizzie craned her neck toward the open door. The library door was closed; the noise had come from within.

"Ignore them," said her mother. "Let me see your work."

Bizzie handed her mother the beginnings of the child's woolen sock, stretched in a triangle between three knitting needles.

"You knit quickly in the round," said Lady Doneraile, taking Bizzie's knitting in her hands. She held it up to the candlelight, examining the inch or so of ribbed material that had already started to grow. "But you slipped a stitch, right here." She used a knitting needle to point out a miniscule hole in the fabric. "Rip it just back to that spot and do it right."

Disappointment niggled in Bizzie. "But you can hardly see it!" she protested.

Her mother looked up at her with stern eyes, the candlelight casting dancing orange on her pale face.

"It's not that you can't see it, Elizabeth. One mistake will affect the integrity of the whole sock. See this." Bizzie gave a pained cry as Lady Doneraile pulled all three needles out, leaving a round circle of loops dangling, in danger of unravelling.

"Mother, no! What are you doing?" she moaned. She tried to snatch her work back, but her mother held it out of arm's reach.

"Stop being silly, Elizabeth. Come look at this." She glared at her until Bizzie sank back onto her seat, her lips tightening. Lady Doneraile stretched the ribbed knitting apart with her thumb and forefingers, then let go. The fabric didn't spring back into place.

"See there?" Lady Doneraile used her knitting needle to point at a barely noticeable break in the pattern. "You accidentally created an extra stitch. You began with twelve, and now you have thirteen. An uneven number of stitches means your knits and purls won't match up in alternating columns anymore. If they don't match up, the sock won't expand and contract like it should. It won't stay on the baby's ankle."

"Yes, I see," said Bizzie, finally understanding. It was imperative to follow the rules—in this case. One small mistake could ruin everything.

"Good," said her mother, and Bizzie watched in dismay as her mother pulled apart her work until it was a single thread of wool. She wrapped it around and around the original ball of yarn, leaving it looking as though Bizzie had accomplished nothing in the past hour.

"Start over," said her mother, handing her back the materials. "We don't want Brigid's baby to have cold feet."

Perhaps in the hopes it would help her find a suitable husband, Lady Doneraile had been teaching Bizzie how to knit and embroider, first having her practice on tattered old tablecloths. She'd been pleased with her progress, commenting on how her daughter had diligently mastered the art of the cross-stitch and the complicated knotting of needlepoint. She succeeded in creating intricate and neat designs on top, keeping the chaos of clashing crisscrossed threads underneath where no one can see. After a few short months of working together, Bizzie had been able to make old table linens look new again.

Today was a special day, Bizzie thought. She'd gotten to spend time alone with both her father *and* her mother.

"Once Brigid's baby is born, perhaps you can

learn smocking," Lady Doneraile said warmly to her daughter. "We could make them a christening gown. I think Brigid would like that."

Bizzie imagined a burbling baby dressed in a gown that she had made. It was a sweet image.

"When can I start working on those silks you ordered from Belfast?" asked Bizzie.

"Not yet. Maybe soon."

Bizzie was eager to start decorating the linens that would fill her bridal trunk. Though perhaps her parents didn't know it yet, she was starting to feel she knew whose bed she wanted to make with them.

Her mind filling with fond thoughts of Richard Aldworth and babies, she smiled as she picked up the baby sock and started over.

Chapter 9

KEEP YOUR EYES DOWN

November 1712

Brigid O'Hanlon crunched through the woods, a basket of freshly cut turf under her arm. It was a chilly day, and she wrapped her shawl tighter about her shoulders as a breeze swept in, rustling the skeletal branches above her head. She suddenly winced in pain as red-hot stabbing burned in her abdomen. The basket slipped from her fingers. She caught it just in time and stopped, leaning against a nearby tree as she sucked in several sharp breaths.

Dumping the basket, she spread her skirts and rested on the grass, pressing a hand on her swollen stomach. It was so heavy now, getting in the way of her work. Through her dress, she could see her baby move around, shifting as it rolled over and wriggled in its rapidly shrinking space. *Is that a foot or an elbow?* She rubbed her belly as the pain faded, beads of sweat on her brow.

"I know you're running out of room, little one," she murmured. "You want out. Shh, I know. Just wait until we get home."

She pushed herself to her feet, almost losing her balance for a moment before planting her feet on the ground. Her stomach was heavy as she carried the basket in the crook of her elbow, taking in slow, deep breaths as her shoes crunched on the grass. The pain had already subsided, but its frequency was increasing by the day. It wouldn't be long now.

Brigid headed home, passing the large boulder in the forest clearing where she'd gotten married less than ten months before.

The Catholic wedding had been held there in secret, deep in the woods on Doneraile Court's estate.

"Don't come," Brigid had warned Lady Doneraile. "It isn't safe for you. It's not safe for anyone."

Although the St. Legers were Protestant descendants of a knight sent to Ireland to destroy Catholic monasteries, all six of them had broken the law to attend Brigid's clandestine wedding.

Brigid had grown up in Doneraile Court and until her marriage worked as a housemaid alongside her mother, Mrs. Casserly. Brigid had only recently learned upon the death of her father that he wasn't her father at all. Before she was born the St. Legers had allowed her mother to live and work on the estate even though she was pregnant and unwed at the time.

A quick marriage was arranged with Mr. Casserly, a Catholic man who assumed the role of Brigid's father and became the St. Legers' butler until his untimely death. The Casserlys were all considered part of the family. It didn't matter that their religion was different.

Lord Doneraile had walked Brigid down a makeshift aisle between the crowd that cold February morning, frozen twigs and frost crunching beneath their shoes as they made their way to the ancient boulder that had served as an altar. Children had decorated the place with paper flowers and weaved baskets, and everything had been covered in a glistening layer of frost.

The Catholic priest's consecration was an uncomfortable affair. When he'd spoken of the body and blood of Christ, the St. Legers and the rest of the congregation had stared at their laps, silence hanging between them. If anyone asked if they'd been to mass, they wouldn't be lying. They had seen nothing.

Brigid, her dress tight-fitting and finer than anything she'd ever worn, had surveyed the crowd, bright brown eyes looking around at everyone she knew. They had gathered to watch her marry Sean O'Hanlon, one of Lord Doneraile's tenant farmers, a good man, if a little hot-headed at times.

Lord Doneraile and his family had stuck out in the crowd of Catholics like court jesters at a peasant market, their brightly colored gowns of finery clashing against the crowd of rags the Catholics considered their Sunday best. The wealthy family had earned more than a few strange looks from the other attendees.

"Aren't I marrying up?" Sean had said proudly to Lord Doneraile when he'd given him Brigid's hand in place of her absent father. The young man's face had shone with joy as he'd gazed upon his blushing bride. If he'd noticed the awkwardness in the crowd, he hadn't shown it, only having eyes for his new wife.

Lord Doneraile took his place between Mrs. Casserly and Lady Doneraile. On the other side of his wife sat Elizabeth, Arthur, John, and Hayes. Hayes kept his head down during the entire ceremony, refusing to make eye contact with the bride at all. Perhaps he was afraid that if he looked up and met her sharp gaze, all the secrets between them would come spilling out.

"That little bastard," Brigid snarled to herself, remembering the agony that stabbed her heart when Hayes refused to acknowledge her that day. He'd certainly had eyes for her the night before.

Snippets of memories flashed through her head—the sight of him with his trousers down, the heat of his breath on her shoulder, and the pain of losing what she planned to save for her wedding night. That pain in her heart was worse than the shooting aches in her belly and lower back right now.

"Hail, Brigid! Do you need a lift?" said a friendly voice behind her. She blinked from her memories and looked up to see Mick O'Sullivan, the St. Legers' gardener. She'd been so absorbed in her thoughts she hadn't heard his horse and cart coming. Mick's old mare stopped before her, shaking her mane as she gave a light snort.

"Oh, Mick! Yes, thank you," Brigid said, clambering into the back of his wagon with some difficulty. He extended a hand, and she grabbed it thankfully, wincing as she worked with the heavy weight of her stomach. She sighed, cradling her belly. "Thank God you're here. You couldn't have come at a better time. I was beginning to wonder whether I'd make it back on my own."

"The little one will be coming any day now, eh?" Mick said, voice jovial as his sea-green eyes flickered to the prominent bulge of her stomach. As though the baby sensed his gaze, it gave another little kick, and Brigid affectionately rubbed her stomach.

"I was just thinking that yesterday," Brigid said, shifting to make herself comfortable on the wagon bed. Mick clicked his tongue, and the horse resumed her steady, slow pace, hooves sinking into the dirt as they rattled along back toward Brigid's cottage. "What are you doing this far away from the gardens?"

"Tomorrow's the full moon, isn't it?"

"Ah, yes," she nodded, settling half on her back, her hand over her stomach. "We'll be expecting company."

"Right-ho," said Mick. "I've made sure all the drives across the estate are perfectly clear of any fallen trees, twig leaves…, and pigs!" he chuckled at his own joke. "All's clear in the north, south, east, and west, just as our fine butler asked."

"Our fine butler, indeed," said Brigid as her abdomen gave another burning twinge.

Chapter 10

THE NOOK

November 1712

The morning of November 13, 1712 began just as any other autumn day at Doneraile Court. Birds twittered among the darkening leaves, fluttering from branch to branch as the sun rose to dry the grass still damp with sparkling dew. Red deer inched out of their dens beneath the branches, ears flicking to and fro as they glanced around for danger, bleating after their young, who jumped from their nests as soon as they awoke.

Like them, Bizzie sprang out of bed as soon as she opened her eyes, unlike her usual habit of lingering among the sheets until someone riled her up. She'd dreamt of Richard Aldworth. Her toes curled in delight at the fantasy of stolen kisses by the river locked tight in her mind.

The wood in the fireplace had burned down to glowing embers, but the room was unseasonably warm. A glance outside at the dew told her it would be foolish to trust the warmth, so she draped a thick shawl over her shoulders and brushed her teeth with the frayed end of a willow twig before heading downstairs, slippered feet padding softly on the polished floorboards. The house was not yet awake, and it breathed like a living thing with the kind of sleepiness that comes at the break of dawn.

She opened the front door as quietly as fate would allow, a cold breeze rustling her auburn hair and banishing the last of sleep clinging to her eyelids. She stepped outside, the grass tickling her ankles, and turned to check the mansion's windows for spying servants. Three floors, each with seven windows across. The servants liked to lurk and gossip, and this morning was no exception. Though the windows on the ground floor were free of people, a thin and weathered woman was watching Bizzie from the fifth window on the second floor.

Mrs. Casserly lifted the windowpane with a grunt but only managed to pull it up a few inches. She crouched, trying to push her face horizontally through the small space.

"And where do you think you're going?" she yelled out. Her hands were cupped around her mouth and poking out on the windowsill while the windowpane was pushing back the white bonnet with ruffled trim on her graying head.

"You're wearing nothing but your chemise!"

And a shawl, thought the girl in indignation.

"I'll be back in time for breakfast!" Bizzie shouted back, and she sprinted down the sloping front lawn before Mrs. Casserly could stop her. She had to check the nook.

The cold morning wind streaming in her hair, the shawl clutched tight about her shoulders, Bizzie ran down the lawn toward a towering chestnut tree along the south bank of the River Awbeg.

The Spanish chestnut was as wide as Bizzie was tall. In fairness to the smaller trees surrounding it, the Spanish chestnut was really two that had fused into one while they had grown from saplings. The trees had twisted around and around each other before breaking apart like two extended arms, reaching for opposite ends of the sky. They grew in contrary directions for a half-dozen feet or so, then abruptly angled back together, as if realizing they missed each other after all. There, the trees fused again like reunited lovers.

"It's like two friends forever frozen in a handshake," Bizzie had remarked when she'd first seen it, much to her father's amusement.

The metaphor made it a fitting place for Bizzie and Rhiannon's nook.

At the base of the tree was a triangular void, a cave-like hole large enough for two people to crouch in. It was the only other place where one could tell the enormous tree had once been two. It was a part of the tree that few people knew about.

Heedless of the dew leaving damp trails on her nightgown, Bizzie got to her knees and ducked inside. She brushed aside a pile of dry browning leaves, revealing two flat river stones leaning against each other, too conspicuous to be natural but unremarkable enough that an unsuspecting visitor wouldn't notice them. Bizzie moved the stones aside to find what she'd been seeking: Rhiannon's wooden box containing the slate and a piece of chalk. Just as she'd hoped, the slate held a fresh message from her best friend.

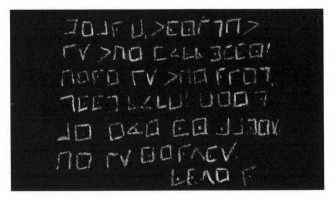

Bizzie deciphered it in her head. She'd dedicated

three full weeks to learning the strange language they used to communicate since Rhiannon's marriage and move to Castle Saffron. With each new message, Bizzie could read it a little faster.

"Dear B," it read in the secret code, "Tonight is the full moon! Here is the ring. Good luck! Keep an eye on James. He is nervous. Love, R."

Beneath the slate sat a golden ring with a tiny heart-shaped locket in the middle. The heart was held by two hands on either side and topped with a golden crown. Bizzie pushed the crown back, popping open the locket door. There was nothing inside it—yet.

On the inner rim of the ring, words were inscribed in the same code. It read: *When you see this, think of me.*

Bizzie's heart thumped. It had worked for Rhiannon. Would it work for her too? Her friend's previous coded messages on the nook's slate had described James as a gentle and loving husband.

Out of a pocket sewn into her nightgown, Bizzie pulled out Richard Aldworth's velvet pouch, the one her father had given her the day she stowed away in his carriage. She carefully placed the ring inside it.

After tucking the pouch safely back into her

nightdress, she erased the message on the slate with some nearby leaves and covered the box with the same two stones. When it was sufficiently hidden, she crawled out of her space to head home. She'd write back in the morning when, hopefully, she'd have some news to report.

Mrs. Casserly was waiting at the front door, her arms folded like a nanny ready to scold a disobedient child.

"What were you doing out there, Bizzie? You'll catch your death of cold," the woman chided her.

"I think I will take a bath this morning, Mrs. Casserly," said Bizzie, making the housekeeper's graying eyebrows rise in shock.

"Well, isn't there hope for her yet?" she remarked as she headed inside to the kitchen, where she'd boil water for her young mistress's bath.

Chapter 11

BRICKS AND MORTAR

November 1712

Lord Doneraile looked in dismay around the lodge room, frustration gripping him. There was no way the work would be completed in time for tonight's meeting. He had instructed his eldest son to supervise the final phase that morning, but Arthur was nowhere to be found.

The hired hands had awaited orders that never came. It had been a tremendous waste of time as they hadn't done much other than mill around and look helplessly at each other.

For the past few months, Lord Doneraile, along with his sons and hired help, had carried several loads of bricks and wood in and out of Doneraile Court's front hall, under the ever-watchful eyes of Sir Ralph St. Leger's portrait.

"Don't worry," Lord Doneraile had said to the portrait as workers lugged in pallets of bricks and housemaids struggled to keep dirt and dust from clinging to the floorboards. "This is all for the greater good."

After a meeting a few months before, Lord Doneraile's brethren had expressed concern about the privacy of their meeting place.

"Anyone could be listening at the library door," said Arundel Hill, his eyes flicking to the oak door.

"We have William serving as Tyler," said Hayes.

"Oh, is he able to be in two places at once?" Arundel's words dripped with sarcasm, making Hayes' eyes narrow.

"The Tyler stands guard in the hall, yes, but this room has *two* entrances from the outside. And this one is in the East!" He gestured toward the library door. "It has to be walled up, or we should find somewhere more suitable to meet."

Nobody wanted to go to the trouble to finding another location, so the group unanimously agreed to remove the door to the library. Now, several weeks later, the door was gone, leaving a gaping hole in its wake. This wasn't good. They'd wanted to close off access to the library, not the opposite. This wouldn't make the right impression on his brethren later.

"How will this look?" Lord Doneraile said to Hayes and John upon discovering the incomplete wall. "And where is Arthur?"

The young men had no answer for him, so Lord Doneraile dismissed his workers and watched with folded arms and frustration in his heart as the last man to leave stopped to put back a carpet that had been furled up in the corner of the front hall. The man, mustached and grunting, heaved the heavy roll up, dropped it, and with a swift, careless kick of his mud-caked boot, sent the carpet rolling out flat. It didn't naturally fall parallel with the door, so the workman slammed his heel into one corner and dragged it *almost* into place.

"Good enough," he grunted, glaring at the carpet like it had insulted him and slammed the door on his way out. Lord Doneraile sighed, rubbing the bridge of his nose.

"I suppose you can't really blame him," he said to Hayes and John pointing to the Persian carpet, it's once vibrant reds and blues now paled with age and footfalls. "That rug was brought over from England by my great-grandfather, Sir Anthony, the one Henry the eighth sent to force the clans to hand over their land to the crown, by force or by choice," Lord Doneraile kept talking as walked over to the rug and straightened it out, brushing out its stringy fibers of wool fringe with his fingertips. "Sir Anthony is also the one who pushed Parliament to declare Henry the official King of Ireland. Until then, the Catholics here considered the Pope their king."

"Looking at all the papists here today, perhaps Sir Anthony only helped to create more saints," Hayes chuckled. There was an amusing kind of irony in it.

"No doubt that man"—John pointed with his thumb over his shoulder to where the workman had excused himself —"prays to several of them."

"No doubt," agreed his brother.

"Let's go and find Arthur. Where is he?" said Lord Doneraile, leading his sons over the precious carpet and out the front door, wondering whether his eldest son was too old for a strapping.

Chapter 12

THE FAIRY TREE

November 1712

Her husband may have been fretting about the hole in the library wall, but Lady Doneraile's mind was focused on Brigid O'Hanlon. She had been in labor for hours now. Her baby was so far refusing to come, leaving the poor Brigid in great discomfort and worry.

The night of the full moon, just a few hours away, would be Lady Doneraile's turn to act as midwife. She was worried things may not turn out well. Women perished from childbirth all the time, and the poor girl was only a few years older than Elizabeth.

"Stable boy," she called, the young boy's name slipping her mind for a moment. "I'm sorry, dear, what was your name?"

"Cormac, madam," said the boy, his cheeks reddening into a blush that made his freckles disappear. "Before you go for the night, fetch me a horse and cart."

Doneraile Court was quiet. Lady Doneraile had given the servants the night off, as she always did the nights of her husband's lodge room meetings. Lady Doneraile was to take herself in a carriage to Brigid's house. Although it wasn't a far walk, there was a comfort in riding a wagon with a horse.

The sun was setting as she settled into the carriage, wrapping her shawl around her. It would be winter soon, and there was a bite in the air.

She started down Fishpond Lane until she came to the curve around the Fairy Tree. The stable boy was setting off on his way home when she hurried him over.

"Wait, Cormac. One more thing. Fetch my daughter, would you? Ask her to bring the baby sock."

"Yes, m'lady." The boy scurried along the road and into the house. Soon enough, Bizzie appeared, auburn hair freshly clean but still streaming free of her ribbon, her boots thudding on the dirt before she clambered into the carriage beside her mother.

"What's the matter, Mother?" she asked as the horses resumed their steady, clopping pace, the carriage rumbling beneath them.

"Your great-grandfather, the knight," said Lady Doneraile. "He wanted this lane to be straight

98

and narrow when he settled on this land nearly a hundred years ago."

"But the Irish wouldn't let him chop down the Fairy Tree," Bizzie nodded. She'd heard this story many times before, first from her mother, then from Mick, then from her mother again.

"Right. They told him cutting it down would bring on years of bad luck, and he thought it best to humor them," she said, her eyes staring straight ahead as they approached the tree. "The folk around here, they believe fairies live in trees like these. That's why it has all those shiny trinkets and ribbons over it. They're gifts, they say, for the fairies, in exchange for good luck."

Bizzie thought there was something rather romantic about the whole thing, but her mother added, "It's silly."

The tree stood glimmering in the evening sun before them. It approached the hills in the west, casting a warm orange glow across the sky, the clouds blown to a scattering of white like smudged paint.

"It wouldn't hurt this one time," said Lady Doneraile thoughtfully, glancing at her daughter. "Give me the sock you made."

Bizzie took out the baby bootie she'd knitted

the night before. She'd checked for more slipped stitches a dozen times before presenting it to her mother for approval. The white thread felt delicate in her fingers, and she held it tightly until her mother's hand wrapped around it, lest a sudden breeze might snatch it away.

They descended from the carriage and ducked under the outer branches of the Fairy Tree, looking up into the innards of it. Not much grew around it other than several wild patches of grass.

"You see that, Elizabeth? The branches are all pointing in the same direction," said Lady Doneraile, pointing to the leafless branches all growing straight out to the east and parallel to the ground.

"It's like it's frozen in an invisible gust of wind," said Bizzie.

Several dozen baby booties hung from the branches, weathered and dirtied from years gone by, swaying gently in the evening breeze. Some of them had pairs; others did not. Lady Doneraile tied Bizzie's bootie onto a branch, taking care not to hang it next to singular socks that had never met their matches. She stuck her hand into her dress pocket, making sure her own bootie was still there.

"When Brigid's baby has been delivered safely

to this world, we'll come back and tie its match to this tree."

Her daughter nodded. Her family may not believe in fairies, but on the off chance they might be real, Bizzie hoped that they would spare Brigid and her new baby. Mrs. Casserly told her how much pain her daughter was in and how long the child was taking to come.

They ducked out from beneath the tree to where the horse and wagon awaited. Lady Doneraile planted a warm kiss on her daughter's forehead, then clambered back into the cart. With a snap of the reins, her journey continued down the lane to Brigid and Sean O'Hanlon's cottage.

It was getting late. The piercing cry of a crow sounded nearby. Bizzie glanced up to see a murder of black birds flapping in the direction of Doneraile Court. They were going home to roost for the night as darkness gathered, and lanterns flickered on in the scattering of houses on the hills. Goose bumps stippled on Bizzie's bare arms as she shivered. Winter was coming.

As she walked toward the house, leaves crunching beneath her boots, more and more birds flew in from all directions, cawing at each other as they landed on the same oak tree near her house.

They squawked, the cacophony of bird calls almost deafening as they performed their nightly ritual.

They took off from the branches en masse, then settled back down again, vying for the warmest spots in the center of the great oak. Their black bodies nearly disappeared in the silhouette of the tree as the full moon replaced the sun in the sky, casting ghostly light on the dirt path.

Unnerved, Bizzie hurried home to prepare for Richard Aldworth's arrival.

Chapter 13

POITIN

November 1712

James Coppinger sighed, staring at his reflection in the looking glass. There a tension in his broad shoulders. A crack sat in the corner of the mirror, gathering dust, and he made a mental note for the fifth time to purchase a new one. He'd spent weeks preparing for this night, his anxiety building the last month as each new drew closer to the next full moon.

He was halfway through buttoning up his shirt when he paused, letting the material slip from the left side of his chest. He touched the spot right above his nipple. Though no harm had yet come to it, the skin felt tender, vulnerable, as though anticipation alone made ghost pains prickle and burn.

"So mote it be," he muttered to himself in the mirror.

"What's that?" said Rhiannon, the creak of the door betraying her presence. His heart still fluttered when she entered the room, the sunlight catching in her fiery hair. Her tan from living abroad had faded, and her dresses were finer than they'd been when they'd first met. James had once considered the idea of asking Lord Doneraile for his daughter Bizzie's hand, but since first laying eyes on Rhiannon, all thoughts of marrying Bizzie had gone straight out of his head. Elizabeth St. Leger was a dear friend, and they would always have their fond childhood memories, but Rhiannon had burrowed deep into his heart with a look. He was happy with the butler's daughter.

"Oh, it's nothing, nothing," James said, continuing to button his shirt. His eyes looked tired, and his skin looked suddenly ashen in color. He rubbed his eyes, forcing a smile when Rhiannon came up beside him, her soft natural scent of flowers and sunshine tickling his nose.

"You're still nervous," she said in that soft voice he loved, reaching to touch his arm as they watched each other in their reflection. Her hair was down today, rippling down her back and chest like a fiery waterfall.

"I wish your father hadn't told me what was going to happen," James sighed, turning away from his wife. "It would be easier, somehow, to not know what was coming."

"He was trying to help prepare you," she followed him. "You should be flattered he vouched for you. He takes the brotherhood seriously."

James snatched his coat jacket off a nearby chair and pulled it on, the tender part of his chest still twinging. How strange that you can feel pain that isn't there when you're anxious. He put on his wig, white and tied with a bow, and checked his reflection one last time.

"Well, I'd better be going. I'll see you soon, my love," he said, kissing Rhiannon on her forehead. "Don't wait up for me."

James descended the circular stone staircase from their bedroom in the tower and left the grounds of Castle Saffron through a small door in a stone wall that abutted Doneraile estate. He followed a well-worn footpath through the trees. Years ago, he and the St. Leger children had trudged this pathway between their homes, making up all kinds of games and chasing each other. This little wood used to be filled with their laughter and jokes. James smiled at the memory. They were simpler times.

As he approached the formidable mansion that sat high on the hill, casting its shadow against the darkening sky, he caught voices in the air. It was Lord Doneraile and his sons John and Hayes, calling out Arthur's name. He came upon the three men as he walked alongside the River Awbeg, looking up at Doneraile Court sitting solemn in the distance on top the hill. Candlelight lit up several of the ground floor windows, but the upper floors were dark.

"What's going on?" he asked them. They were all dressed nicely for the lodge room meeting: ruffled shirts and waistcoats over breeches, though none of them yet wore their powdered wigs yet, nor their short white aprons.

"We can't find Arthur," said Lord Doneraile. "And we need him to make a quorum for tonight's meeting. If we don't have at least seven masons there, we can't initiate you."

"Arthur!" James bellowed. His voice echoed into the night, sending several crows flapping away with alarmed squawks. "I want this over with," he muttered, mostly to himself. He wouldn't be able to handle another month of tension.

"I understand," said John.

They approached the river, their shouting voices echoing across the hills. James joined the trio, wishing he had a lantern to ward off the darkness. He was about to suggest fetching one when a weak, pained voice called out to them.

"I'm here, I'm here. Stop that yelling, for God's

sake."

The four men leaned over the riverbank to find Arthur naked, half buried in mud and water at the edge of the river, groaning with his eyes closed, the muck flowing around his head as he faced the darkening sky.

"Don't laugh," he groaned as his brothers snorted with glee. "It's working. Just a few more minutes, please."

"What's working?" asked Lord Doneraile. He glanced at his sons. "What in the world is he doing?"

"Getting rid of the horrors," Hayes said with a knowing chuckle. But to his father's silence, he explained, "The alcohol."

"Sean O'Hanlon told him that sitting up to your neck in river silt will purge your body of it," John laughed. "Arthur's been at the *poitin* again."

"Isn't Sean the one who taught Arthur how to make *poitin* in the first place?" asked their father. He didn't try to hide the disapproval in his deep voice.

John pointed over to what looked like a cluster of mushrooms near the water's edge. James had to squint to see what he was pointing at. "There are their pots."

"Those are the tops of the lids, aren't they?" said Hayes, approaching them. "Sean says the alcohol ferments better underground."

"How big are the pots?" asked James, fascinated.

"A few gallons each, at least."

"Remind me to come back and destroy them," said Lord Doneraile, not sounding amused at all. "Enough is enough. It's nearly time for the meeting. Now let's clean him up."

Chapter 14

THE MURRAIN STONE

November 1712

Lady Doneraile pushed open the creaking wooden door of the O'Hanlons' thatched roof cottage and was immediately hit by the smell of burning turf and vomit. Brigid was lying on her side in bed, alternating between writhing in pain and heaving in sickness. A clay pot sat nearby, and beneath the other scents was the strong smell of alcohol.

As Lady Doneraile approached the young woman, Brigid groaned and heaved again, spitting into the wooden bucket beside her bed. There were stains of yellowish brown on the sheets. Brigid reached up a heavy hand to wipe her mouth, her eyes flickering, a sheen of sweat on her upper lip. She lay with her legs open, the enormous swell of her belly covered with a thin sheet.

"Sheila, is she…drunk?" Lady Doneraile asked Mrs. Casserly, who was busying herself washing some cloths, her face drawn with worry for her daughter and grandchild.

"Maybe a little," said the motherly servant. "Sean thought a touch of *poitin* might help dull the pain."

"It looks like she's had more than a touch," Lady Doneraile remarked as Brigid heaved again into the bucket with several wet splashes. She wrinkled her nose as another wave of the vomit smell washed over them. "How is she progressing?"

Noting Mrs. Casserly's tight-lipped grimace, Lady Doneraile rolled up her sleeves and took a seat on a nearby stool. Having given birth five times, she felt nothing but sympathy for the girl who'd been in labor for all day. She was wearing nothing but a chemise that clung to her drenched skin, the bottom of the sheet stained a dull brownish red from blood and mess. The blankets were in no better condition. Brigid's hair clung to her face, and when she wasn't throwing up, she groaned in pain, clutching her swollen stomach.

"She isn't," said Mrs. Casserly gravely as she dabbed Brigid's forehead with a fresh cloth. She glanced between the girl's legs and clicked her tongue. "There's still no sign of the head."

"Is it time to send for the surgeon?" asked Lady Doneraile.

"No!" Brigid yelled. "No, no!"

"She won't let us."

A knock sounded on the door. Mrs. Casserly scurried over to open it, the autumn chill pervading the room for a moment as she ushered in the gardener, who took off his hat as he stepped inside. His nose wrinkled at the stench.

"Mick, what are you doing here?" asked the housemaid.

"William asked me to make myself scarce, so I did," said Mick. He approached the bed, recoiled when he saw that Brigid was on display, then seemed to grow used to the idea and perched on a nearby stool in the corner of the room, angled so he couldn't see much more than the top of her head.

"I thought I'd come see how you're doing. I brought some peat for your fire." He lifted a bulging burlap sack.

Brigid wiped her mouth again.

"Did you not see what I was carrying when you picked me up yesterday?" she slurred and pointed to the basket of turf she'd collected herself the day before. "It's drying."

Mick had seen, but he'd needed an excuse.

"Right-ho, well now you have more." He said, picking up the sleán he'd been using to cut turf and started cleaning mud off the blade with a handkerchief pulled from his pocket.

"Where's Sean?" he asked, noticing the absence of the father-to-be.

"He left," said Mrs. Casserly, rolling her eyes. "Said he couldn't take her wailing no more. He said 'I know what to do! I'll be right back!' That was hours ago."

Lady Doneraile shook her head. Men were never much help in these sorts of situations.

The door suddenly burst open again, letting in a wave of cold air. Sean came charging into the cottage, mud clinging to his boots, holding something in his hand. "I have it!" he shouted.

"Have what?" asked Mrs. Casserly.

"The murrain stone!"

A chain dropped from Sean's hand, hanging on his fingers. He held a spherical amulet made of a marbled stone, reddish brown and olive green. It had jagged white veins and was just over the size of a river pebble.

"It'll help the baby come," Sean insisted when no one said anything.

"Where did you get that?" asked Lady Doneraile finally.

"The McCarthys."

"And how much did you pay for it?" she asked, leery of what the Irish believed to be miracles.

"I didn't," said Sean. His face shone with new hope. "I *rented* it."

Mrs. Casserly stared at the stone in fascination as Brigid gave another guttural moan behind her. "Isn't that the stone the McCarthys swear cured their cattle of diarrhea?"

"They say it's blessed." Sean gave a vigorous nod. "Will cure anything. Marty Flynn said it cured his son of the rickets! Here, Brigid, drink this."

He plopped the amulet into a mug of water and guided it to his wife's lips. She took one sip and groaned again, leaning over her mattress to vomit.

'she's too drunk to hold anything down," said Lady Doneraile, helping Mrs. Casserly guide her back into bed. "It's time to send for the surgeon."

"No!" Brigid said, her eyes snapping open. "The baby's coming!"

Lady Doneraile peered between the girl's legs. Sure enough, among the tangle of dark hair and blood was just the top of the baby's head.

"See?" said Sean, grinning as he gripped the cup in his fingers. "I did that! Me and this murrain stone!" He pointed to the cup.

"Yes, yes, Sean. Very good work. Now get

going." Lady Doneraile shooed him off as Mrs. Casserly dragged her stool to the foot of Brigid's bed. "Fetch us a bucket of water and more linens. There's a good lad."

The farmer nodded and followed her directions as Brigid propped herself up on her elbows, fresh pain on her young face. The soon-to-be-mother was ready to push.

Chapter 15

The Night of the Next Full Moon

November 1712

Bizzie arrived back at Doneraile Court, the caws of the crows battling for nesting space still ringing in her ears. As she closed the front door behind her, a deathly silence descended on her.

"Hello?"

No one responded to her shout, so she went upstairs to her room to get ready, following the dim glow of the lanterns. Richard Aldworth would be coming tonight, and she had to be prepared.

Smiling as she thought of how he'd torn that drunkard off her father, she applied powder on her face and put on a pair of pearl earrings her parents had given her for her seventeenth birthday. She reached for the tiny cut crystal bottle of myrrh oil her father had brought back for her from the Middle East but thought better of it. Then she let down her hair, carefully combed it, and tied it up into a neat bun at the top of her head, making her appear taller.

"To keep your hair in place," Arundel Hill had said to her that time he had gifted her the comb. She reached for it and inserted it neatly into place.

She supposed she looked all right, though no matter how hard she tried, strands of auburn hair kept sliding out of place, as usual, and for once – conveniently.

She took a few of the mischievous wisps, braided them, and yanked the strands out. She yelped as sharp pain pierced her temple.

It was bleeding, but she didn't worry. She blotted the spot with her handkerchief. It quickly stopped.

Taking the ring Rhiannon had given her, Bizzie pushed back on the crown. The heart below it swung open on its tiny hinges. She placed the plait of hair inside and squeezed the clasp closed tight with a small click. Using her knitting scissors, she tried to cut the hair poking out from inside but couldn't get close enough to the edge. So, she used her candle's flame to burn off the last of the delicate hairs peeking out from either side of the small locket. The smell of singed hair was strong in her nostrils as they burned into smoke, leaving only a few millimeters of safely guarded strands inside.

Now finally satisfied, she slipped the ring and the scissors into her pocket, her heart pounding.

It was getting dark outside now. She heard an owl hoot in the distance as she approached her bed. From underneath her mattress, she pulled out a book she'd stolen from her mother's bedroom, *The Ladies' Dictionary: Being a General Entertainment for the Fair Sex*. It would make for perfect library reading for the night.

She didn't like to read in her room, and the library had always been hers. She would go there tonight while everyone else was otherwise engaged. There was a certain thrill to being where she shouldn't be. The forbidden book clutched in her hand, Bizzie gently descended the stairs, orange lantern light warming her face as she sneaked to her forbidden place.

"Where are you going dressed like that?" Mrs. Cunnane yelled from below.

Bizzie froze on the stairs. She had been wearing her favorite azure blue dress all day. It was an ensemble better suited for spring than autumn, and she'd wondered why Mrs. Casserly hadn't questioned her about it.

"I can dress how I like when I'm going to meet my husband at the public house!" she heard Colleen, the newest kitchen maid retort and Bizzie's shoulders relaxed. "I don't assume you'd like to join us?"

"Like I'd be caught dead in a place like that," Mrs. Cunnane grumbled in response. Their footsteps faded as they headed out for their strictly enforced monthly visit with their families. Every full moon, Doneraile Court was emptied of servants in favor of the lodge room meetings, leaving a ghost of a manor house behind. When she was younger, the sudden quiet had scared Bizzie. Now she saw it as an opportunity.

Though she was sure the servants had gone, Bizzie treaded carefully, her slippers making no noise on the oak staircase for she always remembered which ones creaked. Her father and brothers should be returning home any moment now to prepare for the lodge room meeting. Bizzie skipped across the floor, excitement at the forbidden act drilling through her as she unlocked the door to the library.

Her poor, foolish brother Arthur had been at the *poitín* again last night, and this morning, he could have witnessed a stampede of horses and not noticed, except perhaps to complain at the noise. It had been easy for Bizzie to sneak into her older brother's room, which stank of urine and vomit, and swipe the key as he'd lain next to his chamber pot, letting out a groan.

"Get me some water, please, Mrs. Casserly," he'd moaned, his dark hair disheveled as he'd half-heartedly attempted to get up, then slumped back onto the floorboards with a pained gurgle. "Please, a fresh jug if you could. No food."

Bizzie had clenched the key in her fist, backing out of his room before running to fetch the servants to get water for her suffering brother.

She would return the key in the morning.

Several lanterns were burning low inside, casting their ghostly glow on the bare bookshelves and the white sheet covering the pendulum clock in the corner. The cushioned seat on the windowsill was still there, of course; it was a place of treasured memories, of reading with Rhiannon and discovering worlds that ignited her imagination.

She locked the door behind her, feeling safer, and stashed the key in her pocket. She scurried over to the windows, closed the shutters, then lit a candle nearby. The room had changed since her last visit, and she looked around with a feeling of sadness.

The pallet of bricks by the clock was gone, but the renovation wasn't yet complete. The doorway had been bricked up, but it looked like someone had run out of mortar a third of the way up. The rest of the void was filled in a clearly temporary way, with bricks gingerly stacked side by side and on top of each other, with nothing but gravity keeping them upright.

Bizzie settled on the cushioned windowsill closest to Doneraile Couts front gate on Fishpond Lane and opened the shutter a crack to see outside. The sun had almost fully set, though the sky was still pale, and the last of the birds fluttered to their nests for the night. She was just about settled when something poked her from beneath.

Wriggling, she pulled out a book from beneath the cushion. It was covered by two pieces of rough wood and bound together with brass hinges.

Symbols were scorched into the wood. The very same, Bizzie realized with a jolt, that she and Rhiannon used to communicate.

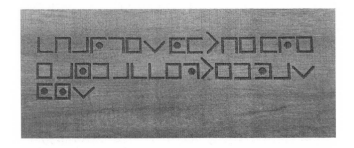

With little difficulty, Bizzie translated it: *Charges*

of the Free and Accepted Masons.

Had the book been left behind by one of the workmen? Rhiannon had never explained how her parents knew this strange language, but whoever owned this book had knowledge of it too.

"Clearly, they didn't follow the rules," she said aloud and startled herself with her own voice. It sounded dangerously loud. She peeked outside, but the lane was bare; there was no one to hear her.

She flipped open the first page of the book. It was unlike usual paper, softer to the touch but strong like leather. On it were inked symbols, all the same secret code she had learned to communicate with Rhiannon. Bizzie was confused. Wasn't this their own secret language? What was it doing in a book?

From the library of Arthur St. Leger, Worshipful Master.

The book belonged to her father.

A gold ribbon hung from the bottom of it. She used the ribbon to slice the thick book open to the marked page. This page, like all the others, was also written in the same code, but Bizzie had no problem deciphering it.

Remember now thy Creator in the days
of thy youth,
while the evil days come not,
nor the years draw nigh,
when thou shalt say,
I have no pleasure in them.
While the sun, or the light, or the moon,
or the stars, be not darkened,
nor the clouds return after the rain.
In the day when the keepers of the house
shall tremble,
and the strong men shall bow
themselves,
and the grinders cease because they are
few,
and those that look out of the windows
be darkened.

"The Bible?" Bizzie whispered quizzically

aloud. She recognized the passage. It was Ecclesiastes chapter 12. Why would something anyone could read in the Bible be written in a secret code? Stumped, she suspected she now knew less about the lodge room meetings than she had that morning. She peered out of the window for any signs of approaching horses. Seeing none, she read on.

And the doors shall be shut in the streets,
when the sound of the grinding is low,
and he shall rise up at the
voice of a bird, and all the daughters of
musick shall be brought low.
Also, when they shall be afraid of that
which is high,
and fears shall be in the way, and the
almond tree shall flourish,
and the grasshopper shall be a burden,
and desire shall fail:
because man goeth to his long home, and
the mourners go about the streets.
Or ever the silver cord be loosed, or the
golden bowl be broken,
Or the pitcher be broken at the fountain,
or the wheel be broken at the cistern.

Then shall the dust return to the earth as
it was: and the spirit shall return
Unto who God gave it.
Vanity of vanities, saith the preacher. All
is vanity.

The passage left a sense of sadness over Bizzie. Perhaps she'd been hoping for something more exciting—secret information, or a map to treasure, perhaps. Instead, what she read felt like a reminder of everyone's mortality, and now she just felt depressed. Frowning at her own childish foolishness, she set her father's book aside. The full moon had begun to rise, the majestic pale orb casting its shimmering light on the flowing Awbeg River.

The moon's silvery shine plus the candle burning beside her made for just enough light to make out the words in something sure to cheer her up: her mother's *Ladies' Dictionary*.

"All is vanity!" she whispered to herself, remembering she was still young and vibrant. Squelching a giggle, she read the first page.

"Is it proper for a woman to yield to the first address from a man she loves? Don't take the first offer you get. The French and Irish soldiers haven't managed to kill off all the good men yet. Besides, you will get better conditions if the enemy does not know how weak you are within."

"How weak I am?" Bizzie whispered. She squeezed the pocket sewn into her dress, making sure the ring with the lock of her hair was still there.

The pendulum clock in the corner of the room ticked, but with her father's protective sheet over its face, Bizzie could not tell what time it was. So, she read on, turning to a chapter about corsets.

"Their bodies, they pinch in, as if they were angry with nature for casting them in so gross a mold," the book read. "But as for their looser parts, them, they let loose."

Bizzie recalled Mrs. Casserly helping her dress that very morning. Tighter and tighter, the woman had pulled the strings of the young girl's corset, ignoring Bizzie's protests that she was crushing her ribs.

"Don"t you want to be married one day?" Mrs. Casserly had asked. According to the *Ladies' Dictionary,* the head housekeeper knew what she was talking about.

"Men do very well know how dangerous it is to look upon a naked bosom," the book read. Bizzie's cheeks warmed. "Vain women know how advantageous it is to show it."

Noted, she thought, closing the book. Bizzie took comfort in being back in the library, her familiar place, among the scent of wood and the candle, the familiar weight of a book in her hands. Her eyelids grew heavy. She lay against the cushion on the windowsill, and although her gaze still moved across the page, she soon fell asleep.

Chapter 16

THE PENDULUM CLOCK

November 1712

Bizzie jerked awake at the sounds of footsteps and voices in the front hall. She peeped out of the crack in the shutter to see a row of horses and carriages outside the house. It was dark outside, several lanterns casting their orange glow on the gardens. A cold chill swept the room. How long had she been asleep? She'd only closed her eyes for a few moments.

Her heart seized when she heard her father's voice, slightly muffled.

"Brother Hill, let me show you the work we've done here in the library."

Her father had his own key. Bizzie sprang into action from her perch on the wide windowsill. She licked her thumb and forefinger and snuffed out the candle, snatched up her blanket under one arm and her mother's book under the other and looked around wildly. There was nowhere to hide other than with the pendulum clock in the corner, covered with an old white sheet.

As her father's key turned in the lock, Bizzie slipped beneath the sheet and opened the clock's cabinet door, turning around and stuffing herself inside, rear end first. She was careful not to stop the pendulum swinging at her back.

She tried to make herself as small as possible, but it wasn't quite enough. Her toes stuck out. The cabinet door could not close all the way.

She'd only just tugged the white sheet back into place when the library door opened with its familiar groaning creak.

"As you can see," said her father, "we've removed everything from this room for renovations, except for the pendulum clock. It keeps perfect time. I didn't want to risk that by moving it. Therefore, we covered it with that sheet to keep out the dust."

From behind that sheet, Bizzie could just make out their silhouettes. Light from the main hall behind them, and the dark shadows of her father and Arundel entered the library.

Bizzie clapped her hand over her mouth to stop herself from breathing too loud, her elbow clutching the fabric of her blanket and pressing her mother's book against her ribs. Her other hand was gripping the just snuffed candle. Hot wax was dripping and hardening on her fist. She prayed her father didn't smell lingering smoke. She was thankful she had the foresight not to wear the myrrh, he'd surely smell that. If he removed the sheet, she'd be discovered at once.

A silhouette she assumed to be her father pointed. "You'll see here we've eliminated the door to the lodge room, the possible breach you mentioned before," he said to Arundel, whose shadow was shorter and wider.

"We're walling it over. As you can see, it's not yet complete. We still need to finish the brickwork and spread the plaster, but it's good enough for tonight."

Lord Doneraile's guest was quiet for a moment, and Bizzie tried hard not to grunt or wince at the cramped space digging into her hips and shoulders. Finally, Arundel's voice broke the silence.

"Your seat will be just on the other side of this wall?"

It was her father's turn to say nothing.

"Worshipful Master?" prompted Arundel.

"My book," said Lord Doneraile.

Bizzie stifled a gasp, a jolt of panic shooting through her, making her stomach hurt and her fingers numb. She'd forgotten to place her father's book back in its place beneath the window seat cushion.

Lord Doneraile's heavy footsteps clomped on the floorboards as he approached the window seat. She prayed he wouldn't touch the padded cushion; it would still be warm from where she'd slept.

"I must have left it out. Strange," he said finally, and she could breathe again. She let out a silent sigh as her heart galloped in her chest.

"How very careless of me." said Lord Doneraile.

"Indeed," muttered Arundel.

"Anyway, Brother Hill, to answer your question, the Worshipful Master's seat will be just on the other side of these bricks, yes. Due east, as it should be."

Bizzie's ears pricked up at that. Due east? Worshipful Master? What did all this mean?

"Spoken like the Great Architect," said Arundel, a mocking tone in his voice.

"Of course, that seat is mine now, but who's to say it won't be yours one day?"

Bizzie winced. Perhaps her father had never quite forgiven Arundel Hill for his abrupt departure that day after giving her the comb.

Horses whinnied outside among the clopping of horse hooves, breaking the awkward silence.

"Come," said Lord Doneraile. "Let's greet our brethren."

Bizzie held her breath as the two men headed out. Her father stopped, and his silhouette turned to glance at the clock. She froze.

"Has that clock stopped ticking?"

Clenching her teeth, Bizzie realized her back had pinned the pendulum against the back wall of the cabinet. She sucked in her stomach and arched her back, balancing precariously on the balls of her feet as her father's shadow approached the sheet, hand outstretched to grab it.

The pendulum fell back into rhythm. His hand fell to his side.

"Ah. I must have *not* been hearing things," he said with a chuckle. "Onward."

Bizzie's heart thundered with a frantic mingle of fear and relief as Lord Doneraile and Arundel left the room, the key turning in the lock. Orange lantern light flared beneath the crack in the door as jovial voices greeted each other among the clinking of glasses. They'd be enjoying their pre-meeting round of cocktails in the front hall. As Bizzie inched one foot from the clock case, her hands damp as they gripped the blanket and candle, the scent of tobacco smoke and whiskey pervaded from beneath the library door.

Being careful not to get tangled in the sheet and bring the whole clock crashing down on top of her, Bizzie pulled herself from the cabinet. With a grunt, she yanked her skirts from the cabinet right as the clock chimed.

She nearly jumped out of her skin at the sudden piercing gong of the chiming clock. She froze like a frightened deer, her heart only slowing when the clock chimed again and again. It chimed eight times total, then stopped. It was eight o'clock, time for the lodge room meeting to begin.

From here, she'd be able to listen.

As the men took their places in the next room with the buzz of voices and the scrapes of chairs, Bizzie crept to the makeshift wall of un-mortared bricks where the door to the lodge room used to be. Crouching down, she slid two loose bricks farther apart, creating a small slit she could see through if she squinted. Inside, moving shadows and the hum of voices sent a thrill through her. Bizzie settled in on her hands and knees to watch and listen.

Chapter 17

THE LODGE IS TYLED

November 1712

With his book now safely in hand, Lord Doneraile greeted the rest of his guests in the front hall as they made their way to the door of the lodge room. Mr. Richard Aldworth of Newmarket had arrived while Lord Doneraile was showing Arundel Hill the library renovations.

"It's good to see you again," said Richard, extending his hand to Lord Doneraile, "Under much better circumstances this time."

"That was a noble thing you did, paying Edmund Synan's debts," said Lord Doneraile. "But you know, he is not a Mason. It isn't your duty as a member of this society to help him."

"Yes, Lord Doneraile, I know that. What I had hoped to do that day, and I believe I was successful, was to help you...and your daughter."

Was it the light, or had Richard's pale cheeks pinkened slightly at the mention of Bizzie? I mean, *Elizabeth*, Lord Doneraile silently corrected himself.

"And how did you do that?" Arundel Hill asked, appearing beside the two men, his eyebrow cocking with curiosity as he glanced up at the taller man.

"It's not important," said Lord Doneraile and, at the sound of approaching footsteps, turned his head. He smiled broadly. "Ah! There is our man of honor now."

He held no resentment toward James Coppinger for marrying the butler's daughter instead of Bizzie—*Elizabeth.* As Arundel Hill had suggested, the girl may have still been a trifle too young for marriage. James' cheeks had a pallid texture to them as he approached the others, the nerves evident on his young face. His father-in-law, the butler, William Simon, was beside him, his face stern as always. James murmured to the others in greeting, looking as if he was ready to vomit.

Three knocks rapped on the front door of Doneraile Court. The first was soft, the second harder, the third hardest. William answered it, the others following behind him into the front hall. They weren't expecting any more guests tonight.

"Is this the home of Lord Doneraile?" rumbled a man's voice.

"It is," said William.

"I am Isaac Rothery. Mr. Aldworth asked me to come."

The two men surveyed each other before shaking hands. With a whispered word, William let the man in.

"Is this the person you told me about last meeting?" Lord Doneraile asked Richard.

"Yes. May I introduce you to architect Isaac Rothery," said Richard. Isaac was a short-statured man with an eager face, and the hat he took off as he stepped inside was longer than most, perhaps to give the impression that he was taller.

"He's building a home for me in Newmarket. It's going to have a most impressive winding oval staircase," Richard explained to Lord Doneraile.

"Yes, it's going to be an imposing U-shaped structure, well visible from all around, with two stone-cut facades and a third—" Isaac started but was cut off.

"Where were you entered and passed?" Lord Doneraile interrupted the stranger.

"In my heart," said the jovial-looking man, making his host smile.

"Indeed, then let us see now. We have our new friend, Mr. Rothery,"—Isaac inclined his head, eyes sparkling— "myself, Arundel Hill, my sons,

135

Arthur, Hayes, and John, and Richard Aldworth. Seven. We have a quorum for your initiation," Lord Doneraile said to James. "And William, our ever-faithful Tyler, will stand guard as his son-in-law is entered into our most esteemed fraternity of brothers tonight. Shall we?"

With the others following like shadows, Lord Doneraile unlocked the door to the lodge room, unveiling his renovations to the whole group for the first time.

"Is all this solid oak wood paneling?" asked Isaac as he spun around looking the room up and down, left to right.

"Yes. Cut from trees right here in Doneraile," said the lord, pride in his deep voice. "It lines the floor, the walls—well, almost." He gave a nervous chuckle, looking at the last of the wooden panels leaning on a loosely bricked wall that looked as if it could easily topple in a strong gust of wind.

"We'll finish installing those last few panels in the morning. As you see, the ceiling is complete," he said, diverting their attention upwards.

The men followed his pointing finger and glanced skyward to find the ceiling lined with the same polished brown wood. There were four black arrows, trimmed in gold. They started joined at the center of the room and extended out to the north, south, east, and west, accompanied by meticulously hand-painted black and gold lettering: *N, S, E, W.*

"John painted the cardinal directions," Lord Doneraile said, marveling at the beauty of his son's craftsmanship.

"The Worshipful Master's chair will now sit along this wall, its back due east as it should be."

"But it's not *actually* due east," Arthur said, his voice slurring ever so slightly. It made Lord Doneraile wonder whether his son had been at the *poitín* again, despite the horrors that had plagued him most of the day.

"Is it, Father?"

Lord Doneraile scowled at his oldest son.

"That's true. I suppose it is slightly off. But as the charges tell us, the symbolism in our rituals is more important than the spaces and places in which we carry them out."

He wasn't going to panic over a few degrees.

"And no one will be able to hear what is said inside this room once it's completed?" asked Richard, once again coming to Lord Doneraile's rescue.

"Yes," said the lord shortly and knocked on a nearby wood-paneled wall.

"Behind this wood is a layer of wool, which muffles sound. Once the former doorway to the library is fully bricked and mortared, we will line it with more wool and secure the wood panels on top and plaster the other side. No one outside will be able to hear a word that is spoken inside this room even if they have their ear pressed against the wall. With that, we should call this meeting to order. Do we have our candidate?"

"We do, Worshipful Master," said John, his own status as a duly sworn member of the group was already borne in blood. The small scar that had now sat for a month just above his left nipple was proof of that.

"All right then. Please take him to the preparation room," said Lord Doneraile, gesturing to a door that was camouflaged among the oak paneling at the back of the room.

James Coppinger's eyes widened, darting from side to side like a frightened animal as Hayes led him across the room and shut the door behind them.

"Let's get started. Be seated, brethren."

Lord Doneraile took the Worshipful Master's seat along the eastern wall of the room. On the high back of the wooden chair was a carved image of a harp and, above that, the main tools of a stone mason, a square, and a compass joined together in an unusual way. The L-shaped square's right angle looked as if it was balancing on its elbow—its two arms outstretched. The compass laid on top. Its two points were facing down, set about forty-five degrees apart. Together, the two tools formed a diamond shape.

"Brother Inner Guard, close the door," Lord Doneraile boomed.

Arthur hopped up and closed the lodge room door to the hall with a soft click. He turned to face the group, unsheathing his own sword, and raising it at the ready.

Lord Doneraile pounded his gavel once on the arm of his chair. "Brethren, assist me in opening the Lodge."

Arundel Hill and Richard Aldworth, the two most senior members in the room, pounded back with their own mallets in unison, the sounds echoing in the room as Isaac Rothery, Arthur, John, and Hayes sat motionless, in silence.

"Brother Junior Warden," said Lord Doneraile to Richard, blue eyes meeting the younger man's hazel ones, "what is the first care of a Mason in opening a Lodge?"

"To see that it is Tyled, Worshipful Master," said

Richard.

"See that duty is performed."

Richard got to his feet in silence, standing tall, the lantern light bathing his powdered white wig in orange. He addressed Arthur who was standing by the door.

"Brother Inner Guard, see that the Lodge is Tyled."

Arthur turned his back to the others and rapped on the door three times. From the other side came three similar raps. Arthur yanked open the door to expose William, their butler and Tyler, standing along in the hall. Without a word, William raised his own sword to them and nodded in solemn silence.

"The Lodge is Tyled," Arthur announced.

Arthur closed the door and rapped on it thrice again. William knocked three times in return.

"Have we any business to attend to before we bring out our candidate for admission?" asked Lord Doneraile, his eyes sweeping the silent group before him.

"I do, Worshipful Master," said Richard, raising his hand.

"What is it then?"

"As you know, I have brought with me tonight Mr. Isaac Rothery, an architect. He has just been to Dublin and has some news that may be of great interest."

"Let him stand."

Isaac got to his feet, and though he smiled at them all, he was wringing his hands as though he was nervous.

"Mr. Rothery, I've been assured by both our Tyler and Mr. Aldworth that you have proven yourself to be a Master Mason," said Lord Doneraile. "However, I require proof. Please give me the sign. And do remember we have an entered apprentice in our midst." He motioned to his youngest son, John.

Isaac lifted his left hand, palm facing up, until it was perpendicular to his waist. He then placed his right hand, palm down, on top of it making the proper sign.

"Good. Now come to me and whisper the Mason's word."

The others were silent as Isaac crossed the room to Lord Doneraile and whispered in his ear. Other than the slight hissing of the burning oil lanterns around them that bathed them in dim light, there was silence.

"Good. You may proceed."

"Worshipful Master. Brethren," Isaac began, straightening and addressing the whole room, "I have just been to Dublin and must tell you about some changes afoot in the Craft."

"What kinds of changes?" asked Lord Doneraile.

"While attending Lodge there, I met a man named Sir Thomas Molyneux. He said he has uncovered some more information about the mysteries and that we give too much information to our initiates too soon."

There was a shift in the atmosphere. Arthur, John, Richard, Arundel, and Hayes glanced at each other.

"How so?" asked the Worshipful Master after a pause a beat too long.

"He said he has found evidence that our Master Mason's word is actually..."—he paused—"Matchpin."

Lord Doneraile leaned forward in his chair. "Matchpin?" he snarled. "*Matchpin*, you say?"

The group of men, all except Richard, laughed.

"What kind of hogwash is that?" You mean to tell me the word that was passed down to me, to my father before me and his father before that, is wrong? That the word Freemasons have been using to identify each other for hundreds of years all over the world is incorrect?"

"That is exactly what this man says, my lord,"

said Isaac. He was glancing around now, like a nervous rabbit hiding in its burrow from the fox. "He is writing it all down and is going to—"

"Writing it all down?" echoed Arundel. "You say this man is a Master Mason, that he has taken the same oath as all of us here, and he's not only discussing our secrets but *writing them down*?" Arundel glanced around the room, appalled. "He should be sentenced to death!"

"He is not the only one," said Isaac. "He says there is a group of brethren in London who are contemplating making our fraternity public. They're considering placing ads in newspapers for new members."

Lord Doneraile scoffed. "To let just anybody in?"

"Not exactly," said Isaac. He looked as though he would rather be anywhere but here. "They claim that by breaking up our initiation into several "degrees," as they call them, it will become harder to become a member. But opening up to a larger field of candidates would mean more funds in the coffers."

"Money," snarled the Worshipful Master. "This is what the Craft has become to them?"

"Worshipful Master," Richard interrupted. "I

have met these men in London."

The men all turned to glance at him.

"They are friends of my cousins in Bristol," he explained. "They claim the old ways no longer serve a purpose, that we no longer need to band together to get men out of harm's way. Times have changed, they said. They claim it is time to use our knowledge to expand in a new direction of science and enlightenment."

"Is there a 'New Jerusalem' that I don't know about yet as well?" asked Lord Doneraile, glaring at Richard. The younger man didn't wither beneath his look.

"Well, no. Not exactly," said Richard, pausing and thinking of his other family members who had set sail and settled in the New World across the Atlantic Ocean. "Yet."

"A 'New Atlantis' then?" asked Lord Doneraile. "We know our work's not done until there is."

"No," said Richard thinking of his desire to visit the Massachusetts colony, where his cousins lived near the growing town of Boston. "I can't, by my own experience, say that there is. But there is potential."

"Could we not look at this as further steps on our winding staircase?" Isaac asked Lord Doneraile.

Invoking the value of the ongoing pursuit of knowledge gave Lord Doneraile pause. There was an uncomfortable silence. The only sound was Isaac's rapid exhales through his nose and the intermittent sizzle of the burning wicks. Finally, Lord Doneraile waved his hand through the air, a signal the conversation was moving on.

"I thank you all for bringing this to light. Richard and Isaac, I think we all would appreciate it if you could follow up with these men and find out more about this so-called new information. In the meantime, the members of this Lodge will continue to protect our secrets and the men who know them, in the pure and ancient ways we have been taught throughout the ages."

"Yes, Worshipful Master," said Richard and Isaac as they took their seats.

"Now to the business at hand," said Lord Doneraile, straightening in his seat. "The admission of our newest brother, James Coppinger. Is the candidate ready?"

"Worshipful Master, there is an alarm at the door of the porch," Arthur, the Inner Guard, piped up.

"What is his name, age, and occupation?"

"James Coppinger. Full Masonic age. Landowner."

"Very good. Admit him upon receipt of the *word*."

Chapter 18

COWANS AND EAVESDROPPERS

November 1712

Bizzie crouched on the floor of the library, pins and needles prickling her feet and ankles, dust clinging to the hem of her dress and excitement pumping through her. Her heartbeat was so frantic it was nearly drowning out the muffled voices she was so straining so hard to hear on the other side of the bricks.

Chair legs scraped back abruptly on the floor, the sound of men pushing their body weights up to stand at attention. They let out heavy sighs as they did, as if the mere motion of standing was hard work. Her father cleared his throat. The familiar cadence of his voice reached her ears.

"Most holy and glorious Lord God, the Great Architect of the Universe, the giver of all good gifts and graces. You have promised that where two or three are gathered in your name, you will be in their midst and bless them. In your name, we have assembled, and in your name, we desire to proceed in all our doings."

Bizzie sat as silent as the Spanish chestnut tree in winter. Why would her father need to pray in secret? She tried hard to calm her nerves as she struggled to understand the strange prayer her father was uttering. She'd never heard anything like it. It sounded holy, but it was nothing like they heard at church.

"Grant that the sublime principles of Freemasonry may so subdue every discordant passion within us. Harmonize and enrich our hearts with your own love and goodness. We ask that this Lodge humbly reflects the order and beauty that reigns forever before you. Amen."

"So mote it be," the brothers muttered in unison.

Bizzie struggled to understand the conversation that came next, but she didn't dare move. Snippets of words came to her, like they were carried away on the wind. She caught sight of Richard Aldworth, tall and kind-faced, and her stomach did a somersault. Her father talked about Adam, Noah and his ark, and the Great Flood. Bible stories.

Is he secretly a Catholic priest? Like the priest who married Brigid to Sean O'Hanlon? She found herself wondering, her thoughts floating to the coded Bible verses she'd found earlier that evening.

With little more than a finger's width of visibility, her view through the bricks was sparse. She didn't want to risk them seeing her, so she crouched, still as a mouse, ignoring the protesting muscles in her thighs, calves, and toes. She squeezed her left eye shut tight to better focus on the open right one. She could only see what was straight before her narrow tunnel of vision, nothing peripheral. But she wanted to see more. On the other side of this brick wall was the room she'd been curious about for a long time, and currently in use for its mysterious purposes, at that. It was terribly frustrating.

With an audible sigh she feared may have been a touch too loud, Bizzie sat back on the soles of her feet and looked up at the fragile wall. She surveyed the loose bricks and decided to take her chances. Kneeling now, with her skirts bunched up under her knees for cushioning, she chose a brick that was jutting out slightly more than the others.

Taking the scissors she had stashed in her pocket, she used the tip of a blade to pick at the right side, then the left, slowly and carefully repeating this pattern until she could inch the brick out with her forefinger and thumb. She spread the five fingers of her other hand gently across the neighboring bricks to keep them from coming out, too. Then she took a deep breath and biting her lip in concentration, she removed the brick altogether in a silent slide. Slowly letting go of her breath, she glanced up, fearful the entire wall would collapse on her.

It didn't move.

Bizzie gingerly placed the brick beside her as softly as she could, not making a sound. She peered through the rectangular spyhole, the scent of burning tallow candles reaching her nose, the smoke stinging her eyes. Excitement ran through her as the scene inside the lodge room revealed itself to her for the first time.

The room was dimly lit by three candles, all placed on a small oval table in the middle of the room. A single log burned in a fireplace at the far end, and the men all sat motionless in armchairs along the four walls. She could see a black and white checkered floor below them.

In front of her, his back to her, was her father. He cleared his throat again and shifted in his seat, blocking some of her view with his back.

Without the brick in the way, she heard much more clearly, and his voice was so loud it startled her.

"Is the candidate ready?"

Bizzie had almost forgotten about James

disappearing into that other back room several minutes before. She strained to see beyond the hidden door as it cracked open at the far end of the room near the fireplace. Rhiannon's husband appeared in the doorway, blindfolded, with his shirt hanging off and a rope around his neck. His lip trembled.

God's trousers! Bizzie cursed inwardly as her heart sprang to her throat. *Are they going to hang him? What did he do?*

He was wearing a pair of loose black trousers, the left pant leg rolled up to over his knee. His white shirt was buttoned halfway up and pulled down on one side, exposing his left arm, shoulder, and breast. Bizzie could just make out several curling light-brown hairs around his nipple. Her cheeks flushed at seeing so much bare flesh of a man who wasn't one of her brothers, but her concern quenched her embarrassment. Her childhood friend looked afraid. Did Rhiannon know about this? Or was she in the dark about these lodge room meetings, too?

James shuffled his feet forward, feeling for obstacles, clumsy in his inability to see.

"Whom have you there?" one of the men asked. Bizzie thought it was Arundel, but she couldn't be sure.

Bizzie's brother John answered, "Mr. James Coppinger of Saffron Castle. He has been in the darkness and now seeks to be brought to light."

"Mr. Coppinger, is this of your own free will and accord?" asked Lord Doneraile, his booming voice startling Bizzie again.

"It is," James said. His voice shook only slightly.

"Is he well and duly prepared?" asked Bizzie's father.

"He is," said John.

"Who vouches for this man?"

It's all so…ritualized, Bizzie thought, adjusting her knees below her, trying not to further disturb the brickwork.

"A Brother," said John, his voice solemn. Bizzie couldn't quite see her brother's face from her angle, just a corner of his gold-highlighted brown hair, but she imagined his gaze was downcast, respectful.

"By what further rights and benefits does he expect to gain this favor?" asked Lord Doneraile.

"Be being a man, free born, of good report, and well recommended," John replied. Bizzie squinted to get a good look at James, who had almost reached the group. His head hung low; his shoulders slumped. In that instant, he looked like a meek and vulnerable child, entirely at the men's mercy.

"It is well," said her father finally. "Teach him to approach the east by one upright step."

James shuffled clumsily until he was facing Lord Doneraile and the wall behind which Bizzie crouched in silence. In that moment, she was glad of his blindfold; there was no way he could see her spying. John instructed James to kneel, and then knelt to adjust one of James' legs and feet.

"He stands with his feet forming the angle of a square," John told his father, "His body erect at the pedestal before the Worshipful Master."

This was all so strange to Bizzie. She had heard the men quote scriptures and appeasement to God, but what she was seeing now looked more like heathen Devil worship. *Is my father Satan?* The thought floated across Bizzie's mind as her heart punched her rib cage like a frantic animal trying to escape.

"*His body erect.*" The words echoed in Bizzie's ears as James' torso looked anything but upright. His shoulders were hunched as though he was recoiling from something she couldn't see. He was shielding himself from something, but what?

"Brother Inner Guard," said her father, turning his head to his son Arthur by the hall door. "Please help Mr. Coppinger."

Arthur tread across the room and took James' shoulders from behind, pulling them back so his posture was straighter.

"James Coppinger," said Arundel, getting up with a scrape of his chair and approaching the trembling young man. Arundel stood several inches shorter than James, but in that moment, Arundel looked the bigger of the two.

"Upon your first admission into a Lodge of Masons, I receive you upon the point of a dagger," said Arundel, putting one hand on James' shoulder and pressing the tip of the knife into the soft flesh of his chest, just above his left nipple.

James flinched, the smallest of whimpers escaping his lips as blood beaded at the tip, traveling in a slow, crimson stream down his breast. Bizzie watched in horror, still as a statue, goose bumps springing up over her arms and legs. A phantom stabbing pain burned across her own skin.

So that's what they did to John last month! It hadn't been an accident. Even knowing her family's condition, knowing that even with the most superficial of wounds, he could die, they'd cut him for this strange ritual. They had let it happen— his friends, her brothers, and even their father.

She didn't want to see any more. Knees aching,

ankles prickling from lack of blood flow, Bizzie rose from her position on the library floor. Keeping her footsteps as silent as possible, she hurried over to the door, feeling ill. She had to get out of there. Go to her bedroom, hide beneath the blankets where she felt safe, and try to get the terrible image of James' bleeding chest out of her mind.

Maybe she should talk to Rhiannon about this in their next coded message Though something told Bizzie to stay silent, to not share the secrets she had learned this night.

Yes, better to forget about it and pretend to be ignorant. Put Mother's book back, get out of her tight-fitting corset, and save the ring for another day. The spell was a foolish idea anyway. It was—

Deep in thought and in her hurry, Bizzie didn't spot the corner of the white sheet covering the pendulum clock that had saved her from being caught an hour earlier. She tripped over it and fell to the ground with a thud, her tangled up foot yanking the sheet off the clock's face. Groaning on the floor, elbow throbbing from where she'd landed on it, she turned in terror to watch the clock sway off balance as the chimes inside clattered and clanged as loud as church bells. The clock was sounding the alarm.

Her heart screaming, Bizzie scrambled to

her feet, pulling her foot free from the sheet and searching her skirt pockets for the library key. With trembling fingers, she unlocked the door as the clock rang and clanged behind her. Nothing on her mind except running, she yanked open the door.

The butler, William, stood there, his blue eyes wide and full of surprise, a sharp sword clutched in his hand, its tip pointing straight at her heart.

It was too much.

She screamed.

It was a bloodcurdling screech that reverberated off the walls. The sound carried on the air far away from the mansion, a cry of pure terror that awoke people from their beds and made them whisper of banshees and demons.

Her head spun. Blackness overtook her vision. Elizabeth "Bizzie" St. Leger crumpled to the floor in a faint.

Chapter 19

THE SCREAMING BANSHEE

November 1712

In the modest O'Hanlon cottage less than a mile away, Lady Doneraile, Mrs. Casserly, Mick O'Sullivan, and Brigid and Sean O'Hanlon all froze as the screaming sound permeated their walls from the outside.

Mick was the first to recover, getting to his feet, knees knocking together.

"That's a screaming banshee," he said with confidence. He glanced around at the others, who sat stunned, then put on his hat, heading for the door. "I'd better go."

Without ceremony, the gardener left. Cold night air washed over them all before he slammed the door behind him.

Lady Doneraile sighed. She was elbow-deep in blood and mess, the baby's head crowning beneath her hands. There was no time for superstitious nonsense.

"She's coming for my grandchild!" Mrs.

Casserly cried, leaping to her feet and pointing at the baby. The head and shoulders were on the verge of emerging, red spilling onto the sheets as Brigid pushed, her purple face streaming with sweat.

"She's coming for your child!" Brigid's mother screamed at Sean, who sat ashen faced.

"What are you people talking about?" asked Lady Doneraile, unable to keep the edge from her voice. She had no patience for children's stories, and now wasn't the time to entertain them.

"He has an *O* name, hasn't he?" Mrs. Casserly yelled, pointing first at Sean and then to the bloody mess between her daughter's thighs. "A screaming banshee only comes for people with *O* names! I told you *not* to marry such a man, Brigid!"

"Everyone stop!" Brigid cried. Her sweat soaked hair and nightgown clung to her skin, chest heaving. "That. Banshee. Is. Not. Coming. For. This. Baby!"

She gave a moan that turned into a scream, giving a final push as the infant slid out. Lady Doneraile caught it and turned it over, peering between its legs.

"It's a boy," she said, but blanched as the infant lay limp in her arms. "He isn't breathing."

"W-What?" Brigid whimpered.

"Give me my son!" Sean yelled like a man

possessed as Lady Doneraile used a nearby penknife to cut through the umbilical cord, the child unmoving in her arms as Brigid let out a dry sob. Heedless of the blood and mess covering him, Sean snatched the baby and poured the glass of water with the murrain stone into a nearby bucket, dragging it along the ground with a stony scrape.

"I baptize you in the name of the Father, the Son, and the Holy Ghost!" Sean bellowed, dunking the baby in the water again and again. On the third splash of water, the infant gasped and spluttered, his feeble, warbling cries echoing around the cottage.

Brigid burst into fresh sobs, holding out her arms for her son. Sean carried the wailing baby over, his own chest heaving and crimson on his fingers, and put him on Brigid's chest. The baby had a cut on his eyebrow, from which blood gushed fast and thick, dyeing her nightgown a dark red that spread across the fabric like a shallow wave on dry sand. The new mother quickly pressed the bedsheet against the wound, and it turned red too. She looked up in alarm.

"Quick, get me some linens!" she cried, holding the sheet against the baby's forehead as he wailed.

"Oh Lord, I must have cut his head on the bucket," said Sean anxiously, snatching sheets from a nearby shelf and running over to his family.

Mrs. Casserly stood watching, wringing her hands, and rocking in prayer. Now the baby was breathing, her shoulders had lost some of their tension, but her stern eyes narrowed as she eyed the flowing blood.

"He's quite the bleeder, isn't he?" Mrs. Casserly snatched the linens from Sean and tended to her grandson, turning the squawking baby over and pressing the linens to his bleeding forehead, making soothing shushing noises.

Lady Doneraile froze. Bleeder. As they cleaned the child up, she caught sight of the strawberry-blond curls already adorning his fragile little head. The cut on his brow still bled, turning everything it touched crimson and making Brigid and her mother glance at each other in fright.

At that moment, Lady Doneraile realized why Brigid had said the banshee wasn't coming for the baby with such conviction, despite being just as superstitious as her mother.

O'Hanlon begins with an O, but St. Leger doesn't.

"Sean, fetch a bowl and some sugar and honey from your pantry," she said calmly, getting to her feet. "I know what to do."

Chapter 20

BLACKBALLED

November 1712

Bizzie's rise into consciousness was like emerging from molasses, slow, heavy, sticky. When she finally forced open her eyelids, she still only saw darkness. A heavy cloth had been stretched across her eyes and tied tightly at the back of her head. She was lying on her side on the hard ground. When she tried to sit up, she couldn't. Her hands were behind her back, tied together at her wrists with a scratchy rope. Fresh panic seized her.

"I think she's waking," said a voice. Arundel Hill, perhaps.

Bizzie stirred, not sure whether the presence of the familiar voice frightened or calmed her.

"Where am I?" she said at last.

"Ask her what she saw," someone whispered. Hayes.

Bizzie wriggled in her bonds, her cheek sliding in a small puddle of drool that had formed below her mouth on the floorboards. She swallowed hard.

Pain pounded at the back of her head; maybe she hit it when she fainted.

"Father, for God's sake, do something!" said John's voice.

"I'll handle this, John, thank you," said Lord Doneraile curtly.

Bizzie expected her father to soften when he addressed her. As his only living daughter, he had always let her get away with more than his sons. She was comforted by his voice, expecting him to command the men to untie her, that this treatment wasn't appropriate for a young lady. But when he addressed her, his voice was cold as steel despite the feel of his warm breath on her cheek.

"Bizzie, what were you doing in the library?" he thundered, the use of her nickname not softening his angry tone. "Why is there a brick removed from the wall?"

"I... I...," Bizzie stammered, at a loss for words. The earlier events of the evening flashed through her mind. Her mother's book. Falling asleep on the window seat. Hiding in the pendulum clock—it all seemed so foolish now. Finally finding her voice, she asked, "Is James all right?"

Gasps rippled through the men. It was strange to be prostrate on the floor, blindfolded and bound, and hearing men's voices above her. She felt like a pig prepared for a roast on a spit.

"Oh God, what did she see?"

"Clearly, too much."

"Get her up," growled Lord Doneraile.

Soft hands pulled her to her feet, the rope around her wrists and ankles loosened before falling from her limbs. They guided her along the floor and pushed her into a chair none too gently. They retied her wrists and ankles with the same scratchy rope, only this time to the arms and legs of the chair. Bizzie let them do it, her mind racing. She had to act the fool and pretend she hadn't seen anything. Her father had never been so angry with her. She'd said too much already.

"Who else is here?" She asked, her head twisting around as though her eyes weren't covered. She was disorientated; she didn't know where her father stood.

"It's none of your business, Elizabeth," someone piped up. It was William Simon. He'd always talked down to her. "Just as our meeting was none of your business. But you clearly have no respect for anyone's privacy."

Shame flushed her cheeks as heavy footsteps approached her. "What did you see?"

She recoiled from the butler's hot breath and spittle landing on her cheek. Fear spilled the words from her lips. "I—I saw Arundel Hill stab James Coppinger!"

There was a silence, and she wondered if the men were looking at each other. The silence made her skin tingle. When she almost couldn't bear it any longer, her father finally spoke.

"Men, it's time we take a vote," said Lord Doneraile.

A vote? For what?

"What do our bylaws call for in a situation like this?" asked Richard Aldworth. Despite her fear, Bizzie's heart gave the tiniest of flickers at the sound of his voice. He didn't sound angry or demanding.

"There are no bylaws," said Arundel Hill, his voice firm. "We only know what is in our oaths. To me, she should be considered a cowan or an eavesdropper. She unlawfully made herself privy to our secrets."

"And whose fault is that?" asked a voice in a sneering tone. It was William.

"Some would say it is yours," said Lord Doneraile. He sounded furious. "Is it not your job as Tyler to guard against cowans and eavesdroppers?"

"Others would say it is yours," said William

smoothly. "Is it not *your* job as Worshipful Master to provide a safe and secure place in which to hold our meetings, as we say, 'far beyond the crow of a cock or the bark of a dog?'"

Bizzie couldn't see her father, but she almost felt him bristle at the butler's words.

"Enough," said Arundel. "We should vote."

"But how?" asked John. "What will the vote decide?"

"We could disembowel her," said Arthur, making Bizzie's guts turn to ice. "Or behead her."

He can't be serious! Is he trying to scare me? If he was, it was working. She wished she'd never approached those stupid bricks in the first place. It chilled her to the bone to hear her older brother, the same boy she'd thrown stones into the river with, talk so casually of murdering her.

"We could bury her up to her neck in sand at low tide and let the waves wash over her," said Hayes. If their voices weren't so grim, Bizzie would have sworn they were joking. Did they take their oaths so seriously that they could so easily discuss killing their little sister?

She listened for her father's voice, her only hope of refuge.

"They are all a means to an end," said Arundel,

sounding thoughtful. "But is that the answer? To kill her?"

"It has worked before."

It has worked before? Hearing her own brothers say these words sent a chill down Bizzie's spine. Had they killed someone before to protect their secrets? Who did they kill?

The answer dawned on her as the blindfold around her eyes fell away to reveal the circle of men glaring down at her. *The butler.* William Simon. Before him, Mr. Casserly, Brigid's father, was their butler until he was found dead in the river. Lord and Lady Doneraile told everyone it was an accident, and no further questions had been asked.

"*A terrible tragedy...*" they had said.

Bizzie tried to surreptitiously slip her hands out from in between the armchair and the coarse rope, but it was useless. Even if she somehow broke free, there was no way she'd escape before the men were upon her. She breathed hard, the now familiar lightheaded feeling threatening to throw her back into unconsciousness. Maybe oblivion would be mercy from this nightmare.

The men looked at her with grim faces, all wearing identical white wigs, ruffled shirts, buttoned waistcoats, and those peculiar little white aprons over their breeches—all except James, who was still wearing the oversized white shirt, which was now stained brown by dried blood from the cut on his chest.

Bizzie had never seen such bitter disappointment on her father's face. She felt small, like a child who'd been caught stealing sweets. She swallowed hard, looking down at her lap.

Arundel, the lantern light shimmering in his goatee, held a small wooden box in his hands. It had a hole in the top with two drawers stacked beneath. He pulled out the bottom drawer; it was filled with black and white beans.

"We will vote as we do with candidates," he said, his voice solemn. His cheeks were even pinker than usual. "In this case, white means life. Black…" He didn't need to explain what black meant.

The box was passed around the nine men as Bizzie could do nothing but sit helpless and watch them decide her fate. If she'd known it would come to this, she never would have gone into the library tonight. *Bizzie, you fool! Why did you let curiosity get the better of you?*

Tears burnt her eyes, but she blinked them away. Each of the men cast a vote, and when the box was back in Arundel's hands, he counted the beans as she held her breath, her heart seizing in fear.

"Eight black," he said grimly. "One white."

Bizzie looked in horror at the men around her. Her brothers avoided her gaze. *Out of the nine men here, only one had voted to spare her life?* Her heart screamed with terror.

"A vote for death needs to be unanimous," said William, and Bizzie's shoulders relaxed somewhat. Her fate wasn't sealed. The butler turned his serious gaze to her father. "But we're voting on the wrong person. I say it is Lord Doneraile who must die. It is because of you, sir, and your carelessness that this happened."

The group of men let out a collective gasp, as did Bizzie.

Is he trying to spare my life, or does he want my father dead? Despite getting along so well with his daughter, Bizzie had never liked William much, and the butler had never shown any particular warmth toward her either. He behaved above his status as butler, a far cry from when he'd first humbly approached them on their doorstep.

"In the day when the keepers of the house shall tremble," Bizzie quoted desperately. "Isn't that what it says in your book, Father?"

"My book?" her father's dark eyebrows

furrowed. "Bizzie, what are you talking about?"

"I found it under the window seat cushion," she babbled, her heart racing. Somehow, she felt if she could keep them talking, it would prolong the time until her potentially deadly punishment. "It had your name on it."

The men shifted until Lord Doneraile finally said, "Bizzie, that book is written in cipher. How do you know what it says?"

Bizzie hesitated. They had all just discussed killing her as though it was nothing at all. Would William be as open to murdering his own daughter for her knowledge of their secrets as her family was, apparently, to killing her?

"Speak!" her father thundered.

"It was R-Rhiannon!" she whimpered.

"How does Rhiannon know cipher, Bizzie?" he glanced at William, who stood stone-faced.

"She said her father taught her." Gazes shifted to the butler. "She taught it to me. We—we've been using it to leave messages for each other. That's all."

"William?" her father rounded on the butler, who had blanched. "Is this true?"

"It is," said James with newfound conviction.

The men all turned to look at their newest

169

member. He held his hand over the cut on his chest, red bleeding between his fingers. "He...told me secrets too. Said they were to be kept within the family."

"Is that why you were cowering?" asked Arundel, folding his arms. "You knew what was going to happen."

They all jumped when the library door suddenly slammed shut, and the lock turned with a jingle of a key ring, trapping the men in the room.

As though on cue, William gave a low growl and unsheathed the sword at his hip with a steely rasp, raising it before him as the others stared in surprise. Bizzie froze in her seat.

"William?" said Lord Doneraile, eyeing the blade. "What are you doing?"

"I needed James to become a Freemason to protect my daughter from the likes of you," the butler snarled, holding the blade before him toward Lord Doneraile. Bizzie's father raised his hands, swallowing as the end of the blade neared his throat. "St. Legers, who steal land from its rightful owners and rape Irish brides!"

Shock rippled around the room as Arundel backed away, his ruddy face turning green. Bizzie squirmed in her bonds, hating how close the

170

butler's sword was to her father's neck. James' face was full of confusion, as though he struggled to comprehend what was happening. William's gaze moved to Hayes, who swallowed, fingers twitching as he reached for the dagger at his belt.

"I saw what you did to Brigid O'Hanlon in the stables the night before her wedding," he growled as Hayes' lip trembled. "And I know what this family did to mine."

Lord Doneraile recovered first, though Bizzie could see the tension in her father's shoulders.

"William, calm down," said Lord Doneraile, the fear that had flashed across his handsome face melting away as he regained control. "What are you talking about? I took you and your daughter in and gave you lodging and pay!"

"On land that is rightfully mine!" William spat. His usual composed demeanor was gone, replaced with something vengeful.

"This was Synan land!" said Lord Doneraile.

"That's right. My name should be William *Synan*, not *Simon*. But we lost our name too when we were Barbadozed," said William.

Lord Doneraile knew what the term meant.

But before he could say anything Arthur, as if suddenly realizing as Inner Guard he too had a weapon, took a quiet step toward William, blade raised in the air, hands on the hilt, shaking.

The butler rounded on him, the sword swiping the air with an almost musical swish. Bizzie's brother backed away, hands raised. His sword crashed to the ground.

"My grandfather was a Freemason, just like yours," he cocked his head toward Bizzie's brothers, who grimaced as William picked up and sheathed Arthur's sword to his own side. "Yours could have helped mine back then, but he didn't. Yours watched as my family was sent overseas to work like slaves!"

Moving with the frantic excitement of a man in power, William crouched before Bizzie. She recoiled in her chair with an involuntary whimper, a tear sliding down her cheek.

"I knew you'd foul up eventually, St. Leger," William whispered, his cold blue eyes meeting Bizzie's, but addressing her father. "That I could then take away what you most hold dear."

Bizzie's whimper became a low moan of fright as he pressed the tip of his sword at her throat, the cold steel sharp against her neck. One movement, and she'd be dead.

"William, don't—"

CRASH.

A sudden avalanche in the room was deafening and terrifying.

A cloud of brick-red dust rose where the makeshift wall to the lodge room once stood. Mick O'Sullivan pushed through the rubble, his eyes wild as he quickly summed up the situation in the room. In his hands were the formidable gardening shears that he kept sharpened to a fine edge—blades that no man would ever want to meet for anything other than their intended purpose.

William snarled and gained his feet, holding his sword up as Mick crashed into him. Bizzie screamed, recoiling in her chair as the men shouted, Mick and William scuffling on the ground. Arthur ran forward to help, then leaped back as William's sword almost sliced through his leg. The shears opened and closed with frightening snipping sounds as Mick wielded them with expert precision to keep his opponent at bay. Bizzie didn't know whether to watch or just listen to the fight. Terror kept her frozen in her seat, her eyes wide open as the men brawled dangerously close to the pendulum clock, moonlight shining ghost-pale on their rolling bodies.

Mick yelled in triumph as he straddled the butler

173

and buried his shears into the man's stomach. William gasped in pain, eyes widening as he stared down at his abdomen, red bleeding onto the metal protruding out of his body. as he shuddered and gasped in shock.

Hayes kicked the dropped sword away, sending it scattering across the floorboards as Mick rolled off the butler, his chest heaving. William's feeble hands pushed at the shears buried in his guts as the scent of coppery blood filled Bizzie's nose, churning her stomach. Face parchment-pale, with a ragged gasp, William lay still in a growing pool of blood.

Everyone looked on in stunned silence as crimson ran across the library floorboards, William's unseeing eyes staring straight at Bizzie. She didn't realize she was crying until hot tears dripped from her chin and onto her dress.

It was the gardener who recovered first. Breathing hard, limbs shaking, he got to his feet, blood on his shirt and mud-stained pants. Several of the men backed away from him.

"I'll bury this," he said, grabbing William's lifeless body by the back of his jacket. Yanking out the shears with his free hand and spattering fresh scarlet onto the dusty floorboards, he dragged the body to the door as the others could do nothing but watch.

Chapter 21

WITCH'S BREW

November 1712

No one noticed James Coppinger backing away from the bleeding butler and his killer, where he slipped through the broken wall, almost tripping on some fallen bricks, and fled Doneraile Court. The icy air, verging on winter, pierced his face as he ran, the oversized shirt flowing behind him, clutching the wound on his chest as he inhaled great gulps of ice-cold air that stung his lungs and stung his cheeks.

Despair spilled through him. He had been used as a pawn for William Simon's petty revenge. He'd been a fool. He had never wanted to be part of that strange group of theirs, instead letting his father-in-law talk him into it. Now he had taken their insane oath. He was trapped. They'd spoken about killing Bizzie like it was nothing. Frightened and caving under pressure, he'd voted for her death with a black bean as well, but he'd never thought they would actually do it.

Surely, Rhiannon didn't know anything about this. She loved him. Their wedding hadn't been part of the butler's mad plan…had it?

He had to know.

He ran past the half-hidden poitin pots and along the gurgling river and into the woods, slits of moonlight lighting his way as he fled back to the haven of Castle Saffron. He scrambled up the tower's circular staircase and barged through the door to his and Rhiannon's bedroom, anger screaming in his veins, expecting to find his wife asleep in bed.

Instead, he stopped at the threshold, his pulse pounding in his neck and the scent of rum and candlewax burning his nostrils.

Candles burned around him, hundreds of them, taking up every square inch of flat space in the room: bed, chest of drawers, and chairs. Several sat on the ground, glowing like lanterns at Christmastime, casting their heat on his skin, yellow light flickering on the wood. Rhiannon was in the middle of the room, inside a circle of black powder, and although there was no music, she was dancing, feet thumping the floor in a rhythmic beat.

She wore a dress of yellow and green with bright purple ruffles, a colorful remnant of her life in Barbados. She waved her arms as she spun, her flaming-red hair down and waving like a fiery waterfall with each turn she made, her back to the door. Her bare feet kept their stomping rhythm, and though they danced and flurried, they never disturbed the items that lay on the ground around her feet: several bowls bearing money, tobacco, and flowers.

James could only watch in morbid fascination, sweat glistening along his brow and his chest at the stifling heat of the candles.

When Rhiannon finally turned to face him, the candlelight shining on her face, he could only see the whites of her eyes.

Terror seized the young man. The black powder, the candles, his wife's insane dancing—it was like black magic. She looked like she was in a trance. Everything suddenly made sense. William Simon's betrayal, Bizzie's eavesdropping, and his own sudden, inexplicable fascination with the young woman before him, something that had led to their rushed wedding and many nights where he'd lain awake, his fingers entangled in her red curls, wondering how he had fallen in love so quickly, so easily, when it was Bizzie he was supposed to have chosen…

"You witch," he snarled, stepping into the room. Twigs and mud stuck to his shoes, leaving brown footprints on the floorboards. "What did you do? What *are* you doing?"

What terrible magic was she performing now? Who would die next at her command? Confusion battled fear in James' heart. Had he ever loved her at all?

"Shh," she said, holding up a finger as her feet danced. "You will disturb the Loa."

He reached for one of the bowls at her feet, but she swatted him away. "No! No, no. That's not for you."

Fury building in him, he stepped across the black powder circle and grabbed his wife by the shoulders. "Is this all your doing? You tricked me! You tricked all of us! And now your father is dead!"

She gave a shrill scream like a woman possessed, squirming as she tried to get away, but James held fast to Rhiannon, grabbing her by the waist. His eyes burned with the stench of rum and candlewax, anger and despair fueling his strength as he carried her out of the room and up to the turret of the tower, where the cold fall air rippled their clothes and reddened their cheeks.

"Let me go, James!" Rhiannon screeched,

beating at his arms as he dragged her up to the top, making slow progress up the stone steps as his wife squirmed in his arms. He'd seen death tonight. Heard a man and his family talk of executing his young daughter like it was nothing. Perhaps worst of all, he had been manipulated and controlled by the woman he'd loved and led on by her wretched father.

"It's over, Rhiannon," he said, looking down at the darkness below. "Or it will be soon."

The tower's parapet was half-collapsed on one side. The empty space allowed the wind to roar at him and blow his hair astray as dizziness struck him at being up so high. The ground was dark far below, the river gurgling somewhere nearby, the faint lights of Doneraile Court just beyond the trees. The branches, skeletal and void of leaves, reminded him of Death's hands, beckoning them both.

"James, no!" Rhiannon cried as he put her down and gave her a hard shove. For a moment, her arms pinwheeled, green eyes wide open in shock over her husband's betrayal. Then she fell, hair streaming, to the darkness below with a high-pitched shriek. James straightened his shirt, tucked an errant strand of hair behind his ear, and, before he could lose his nerve, jumped after her.

Chapter 22

So Mote It Be

November 1712

"It looks like the gardener took at least one decision out of our hands," said Arundel Hill. He had recovered first after they'd all watched Mick stomp out of the library, grunting as he dragged William Simon's corpse, leaving a trail of the deceased butler's blood behind. Ice-cold horror pinned Bizzie to her seat. *Oh no. Oh, poor Rhiannon.*

"'While a man thinks himself yet ascending to even greater achievements, the scythe of time will surprisingly end his life and his labors on this earth will suddenly cease'," Isaac said shutting the door. The men in the room all seemed to recognize the quote, Bizzie did not.

"Indeed. But we still need to decide how to deal with the young lady here," continued Arundel, as though the question of her *eavesdropping* was still more shocking than witnessing a murder. "We should vote again. Black for death, white for life."

"Where did James get to?" asked John, looking around. James had disappeared, perhaps to stumble outside to vomit after the gruesome display. Nausea churned in Bizzie's stomach too.

"There's no need for him. He was barely a brother," said Arundel, waving a dismissive hand.

"Let's vote." Lord Doneraile's faced had paled, but he stood with his shoulders back, as though Arundel's words had reminded him that *he* was their leader.

Once again, the men passed the ballot box around their group, depositing the beans to cast their vote as Bizzie trembled, awaiting her fate. When they'd finished, her father poured the contents of the drawers into his palm.

"Six black," he said. "One white."

Again, out of her four family members in this room, three of them had sentenced her to death. She glared around at the group, hating them all and herself for this horrible situation she was in.

Nothing had changed without William and James. All but one person wanted her dead. She looked to her father with pleading eyes. The room swam around her; she wanted to faint again. She forced down the bile that crept up her throat.

"The vote must be unanimous to carry out the

death penalty," said Arundel, impatience tinging his voice. He rounded on the Worshipful Master. "Lord Doneraile, I know she's your daughter, but she saw—"

"It wasn't me, Arundel," said Lord Doneraile, pain etched on his face as his fists clenched. "I cast a black bean."

Bizzie's heart shattered into a hundred bleeding pieces as she glared up at her father. Her eyes shifted to her brothers, who all hung their heads in shame when Arundel cried, "Well? Who was it then?"

John, Arthur, and Hayes eyed the floor like children caught lying.. Four family members, men who were supposed to love and protect her, had all voted for her death. Even John, who'd said he wanted to save her. In that moment, she hated them all. A sob was building in her throat when someone broke the silence.

"It was me," came a voice from the outer perimeter.

Bizzie looked up to see Richard Aldworth step forward to stand in the middle of the circle.

Bizzie gazed up at him, her hatred melting away and turning to affection as heat blazed across her cheeks. All those times she'd daydreamed of him, fantasized about the possibility of courting him—

did he feel the same way about her all this time?

I owe you my life.

"There is another option," Richard said matter-of-factly. Arundel made an impatient noise as they all turned to stare at him.

"Well?" Arundel spat.

"Don't our vows call upon us to *square* our actions? Aren't we supposed to do good unto all? Even if no one ever finds out what happened to this girl, we will know in our hearts that this is wrong."

The men sat silent as Richard continued.

"What is her crime? Yes, technically she is a cowan and an eavesdropper. But who among us hasn't sinned?" The men all shifted their gazes away from him.

"William – we can start with him. I think we can safely say he has broken nearly every one of the morals of Freemasonry. Perhaps, he got his just desserts. James certainly had misplaced faith. But what about you, Arthur?" He turned to Bizzie's brother who was wishing he'd stashed a flask in his pocket.

"You are not exactly a model for temperance. And how about you, Hayes?" Hayes' face blushed redder than his hair. "If what William said is true about Brigid, you could work on virtue."

"John – you allowed your skin to be cut knowing you are a bleeder? That wasn't very prudent. And Lord Doneraile – you let that happen. To your own son. Then tonight you voted to put your own daughter to death. Over what? Embarrassment? Did you let Arundel Hill shame you into thinking your lodge room was not secure enough?"

"What- me? Clearly this situation could have been avoided if—" Richard cut Arundel off. "Arundel, you could work on your mercy. And maybe also jealousy."

"Hear, hear." Isaac agreed with his friend.

"And Isaac, you're a great architect but not the Great Architect. It would behoove you to keep in mind that you are no better than the rest of us. Plus, your everyday use of compasses should have reminded you of the boundary between good and evil."

Richard was really worked up, sweat was streaming from his temple. He tore off his wig and used it to mop the sweat off.

"And I – I am sure I am guilty of all of these things over the course of my life," he said looking squarely at Bizzie as if making a confession. "But now I pray that we have the fortitude to do the right thing."

"Therefore," he said, straightening his back and addressing the group again, "I vote that we put her through the paces. Swear her to secrecy. I vote we make her one of us. the First female Freemason"

Her mouth fell open.

Isaac, who had been so open change previously in the night, made a noise that sounded like a pig snorting. "But *this* is a fraternity of *men,*" he articulated. "It has been that way since the beginning."

John's gaze had snapped up at Richard's suggestion, and he looked around at everyone with fresh hope in his eyes.

"If we do this, then what? Do we allow her to come to our meetings?" He swallowed as he glanced at his sister. She glared back, wishing she could burn him with one withering look. "A girl…a woman?"

"Well, yes," said Richard, as though it was obvious. "If she so wishes."

Richard was throwing her a lifeline. Her heart pounded beneath her frock.

"This is highly unorthodox," muttered Arundel, shaking his head.

The tension in the room had defused somewhat and Lord Doneraile finally had a moment of clarity.

"Richard is right. We are obligated to make decisions based on our own moral convictions and have the strength to adhere to them, regardless of the consequences. None of us, including my daughter, were born into this life fully formed, but through intentional effort we can become better than we first were. She deserves that chance, too. Let's vote on this," said Lord Doneraile and handed the beans to all the men again.

They were no longer voting on her life. The tension in Bizzie's shoulders relaxed, though fear still prickled on her skin. She badly needed to use the chamber pot. It felt like a lifetime before the final bean finally clattered into the drawer and the ballot box was handed back to her father.

He shook the beans into his hand. White. Another white. Every single one of the small beans was pale. Bizzie let out a breath, wanting to sob with relief.

"So, we make her a Mason?" Arthur asked, like he couldn't believe it.

"We must ask her first. Isn't that right?" Bizzie swore she saw Richard's lip twitch.

The group shifted; traditions were traditions, even in the most unusual of circumstances.

"Bizzie," said her father, then cleared his throat.

"Elizabeth. Do you choose, by your own free will"—there was a pause, and the unspoken remark hung between them; none of this was about free will— "to be a part of this—ahem—fraternity of Freemasons?"

Bizzie wasn't sure she'd understood the question, nor what being a Freemason involved, but anything was better than death. "Yes, I do."

Richard crouched before her and untied the bonds around her ankles. "Then first, she must take the oath. She can take James' place for the rest of tonight."

He untied her wrists next, and despite everything, a thrill ran through her at Richard's gentle fingers on her skin. She avoided his gaze, her heart still pounding, torn between her desire to curl up in defeat and her primal instinct to run.

"And from there on,"—he was close enough she felt his warm breath on her cheek, and she looked up to meet his eyes. They were a lovely hazel color, flecks of green among brown. Warmth smothered her fear as heat flushed up her neck—"I will be responsible for her *for the rest of my life.*" He looked at her placing his hand on his heart.

Bizzie's head swam as the others muttered in unison, "so mote it be."

Chapter 23

PREPARING THE CANDIDATE

November 1712

Richard took Bizzie's hand and led her out of the door of the library and into the hall, where lanterns burned low and cast strange shadows along the walls. She felt unwell. She was tired, she still needed to empty her bladder, and shock and nausea gripped her. She had faced death tonight, seen the butler stabbed to death, and had been threatened and betrayed by her own family. The only reason she wasn't bleeding out or drowning right now was because of this man before her.

"Aren't we going in there?" she asked in surprise as they passed the lodge room door.

"Yes, we are, but not quite yet…and not that way."

Richard stopped before the portrait of Sir Ralph de St. Leger. He ran the fingers of his free hand along the bottom of the frame before there was a loud click and the portrait swung forward. Bizzie watched in astonishment as the painting opened like a door and revealed a small windowless room the young woman had never known existed.

A single candlestick burned low in the center of the room, and on the pegs on the wall hung a pair of old black trousers, a plain white shirt, and a rope.

"When a new candidate is initiated, the first order of business is ensuring that his—or her, in this matter—pockets are empty of metal of any kind. Though I can't imagine a lady like you is carrying many coins on you or a knife or sword, for that matter." Richard laughed.

"No, but I do have this," said Bizzie, handing him the key to the library from her pocket.

"Well, this explains *that* mystery," Richard said, chuckling while imagining her tiptoeing into the library with a stolen key.

"I took it from Arthur while he was drunk. I also have these," Bizzie said pulling out her tiny scissors, "and this," she said taking the velvet pouch out of her pocket. She wondered if Richard would recognize it was his, and she flushed as she fumbled with the strings to pour out the golden ring with her hair inside.

"What is this?" he asked with interest, plucking the ring out of her palm.

"Don't touch it!" she said in a panic, trying to get

it back. He held it high out of her reach, examining it in the faint candlelight. "It has a spell on it."

"A spell, hmm?"

"Yes! It was meant for—for you. Rhiannon used the same spell on James. I was…" her voice faltered, a mortified blush creeping up her neck as his soft hazel eyes met hers. There was no accusation in his face, only interest. "I was going to use it on you so that you'd fall in love with me." It sounded ridiculous now that she said it aloud, a child with a fanciful dream. Her voice trembled as she said, "It has a lock of my hair inside."

She could have sworn she saw his mouth twitch in amusement. He snapped open the locket, where several faint strands of her auburn hair nestled inside, then closed it with a soft click.

"I've seen these in Claddagh," he said, looking at the ring in which two hands held a heart topped by a crown. "Wearing the heart pointing out means you're looking for love, and if it points inward, it means one's heart is already taken."

He looked at her, their eyes meeting as she whispered, "Yes." Butterflies took wing in her stomach. The way he watched her made her feel like a foolish, lovesick child. But there was something deeper there too. A rush of heat in her belly, sending tingles through to her fingertips and toes. He stepped closer, and she could sense his scent: leather and horses, with something masculine beneath.

"I see there is something written inside." Richard held the ring up what little light there was coming from the sconce on the wall. "When you see this, think of me."

Richard could read cipher, too.

His warm breath caressed her forehead as he said, "I'm afraid I don't believe in spells."

He slipped the ring onto his little finger. It barely reached halfway, looking comical, but the heart was clearly facing in. He took her chin and slowly tilted her head up as her cheeks burned and her heart sang.

"Besides," he murmured, "it's already too late."

He leaned in, gentle and strong, protective, and vulnerable, and his soft lips met hers. A tear fell from her cheek as she shyly opened her mouth to his, feeling the kiss burn on her lips as a thousand emotions crashed into her at once. He was gentle yet fierce, his arms wrapping around her waist as he pulled her close to him.

The spell was shattered when there was an insistent knock at the door. Richard drew back and his lips parted, leaving tingling warmth on Bizzie's mouth.

"Are you ready in there?" It was Bizzie's brother John. "The sun will be coming up soon. We don't have much time."

"Yes, just a moment." Richard cleared his throat as he snatched the black pants off the peg and handed them to Bizzie. "Put these on under your dress. I'll turn around."

She kicked off her underskirts and yanked them on, feeling the loose cotton hug her hips beneath her frock. When she was finished, he knelt to roll up her pant leg above her knee. He looked up at her.

"Is this dress very important to you?" She looked down at her beautiful azure blue dress and lying, she shook her head no. Richard pulled a knife from his pant leg and, pulling the fabric taut, sliced it in half about mid-thigh. He tore it apart at the side seams, exposing her legs from the knees down. She struggled against the desire to fidget; no man except her family had seen anywhere above her ankles. Then he handed her the white shirt. If he was uncomfortable, he didn't show it. His kiss still burned on her mouth.

"Put this…" He tilted his head, looking confused. "I think over your dress will do."

The man's shirt was so large it slipped over her

head and off her shoulders. Richard asked her to pull out her left arm.

"Your left shoulder and…um, breast need to be exposed. I'm not sure what to do here." He looked at the capped sleeve of Bizzie's dress.

"I'll handle this." She ripped the stitches connecting the satin sleeve to her bodice and tossed it to hang down her back. Her left shoulder was now exposed, stippling with gooseflesh despite the warmth, as was the top of her breast—Mrs. Casserly's handiwork with the too-tight corset.

Richard's eyes lingered for a heartbeat before he turned to pick up the nearby rope from the wall. "This part…is a little scary," he warned, looping it over her head. "This is your cable tow. It needs to be wrapped three times here about your neck."

The added weight of each coil of rope made fresh uneasiness wash through Bizzie, even as Richard worked gently and ensured the material didn't touch her throat more than necessary. She'd watched a convict be hanged in Cork before and knew what a seemingly innocent piece of rope could do. Her throat tightened of its own accord, and she fought the fear bubbling up in her chest. She could be brave. She had faced death tonight.

"There's one more thing," Richard said, holding

up a strip of black cloth. She turned around obediently, and he tied it over her eyes. Once more, she was plunged into darkness.

Chapter 24

BRIGID'S BABY

November 1712

The sugar and honey mixture had worked, just like Lady Doneraile knew it would. The cut near the baby's eye had mercifully stopped bleeding, and the room was silent aside from the tiny gulping sounds of the baby boy suckling at his mother's breast. Brigid held her son in her arms, enraptured by him, stroking his pudgy little cheek as she smiled and murmured nonsense to him.

Sean sat in a corner, his head in his hands. Lady Doneraile had not voiced her fear—no, not her fear, her *knowledge*—that the boy before them was not his son, but he seemed to have guessed it by himself.

Mrs. Casserly stared out of the window at the full moon, her hands scrubbed clean of blood, arms folded against her chest, with a shawl wrapped around her. The smell of vomit and blood still lingered in the small cottage, the fire no one had bothered tending to rapidly dying embers.

Lady Doneraile watched the baby and his mother, knowing one of her sons had done something unforgivable. The infant's hair was the same strawberry blond as her son Hayes'. *Foolish, foolish boy. What have you done?* Lady Doneraile reached in her pocket and squeezed the bootie she knit for the baby. She'd planned to tie it next to its match on the fairy tree on her way home but now feared this infant was not out of the woods yet.

Chapter 25

REBIRTH

November 1712

The door opened with a faint creak as Richard took Bizzie's hand again, leading her into the room. Finally, she had made it into the lodge room, not that she could see anything with the blindfold. She breathed through her nose, willing her heartbeat to ease.

"Whom have you there?" said her father's deep voice.

Richard replied. "One in darkness who wishes to approach the light. They wish to receive the rights and privileges of Freemasonry, as many good and true men have done before."

"How does he—she—hope to obtain those privileges?"

"By the help of God and the tongue of good report," Richard was still holding her hand, and she swore she felt his thumb caress the back of her hand for a heartbeat. "She is a free woman, living in good repute amongst her friends and neighbors."

"What is her name?" asked her father.

"Bizzie St. Leger," came Richard's reply.

"No," said Bizzie, and though she couldn't see them, she felt several pairs of eyes turn to look at her. "It's Elizabeth."

Chapter 26

THE BLOOD OATH

November 1712

Though she couldn't see, Elizabeth somehow recognized Arundel Hill's heavy footsteps as he stepped before her. She thought of the knife, of her brother's bleeding chest, and the chill across her bare shoulder. Remembering James' cowering posture, she stood with her back straight. Richard's fingers slipped from her grip, and for a strange moment in the darkness, she felt alone.

"*Elizabeth* St. Leger," said Arundel, his voice grim as though he didn't think much of any of this. "We believe that for the first time in your life, you now stand within a Lodge of Freemasons in which the brethren are engaged in their particular labor."

She wasn't sure what that meant, so she said nothing.

"By the direction of the Worshipful Master, I have to put to you certain questions. We expect straightforward and truthful answers."

She swallowed; her throat was suddenly dry.

She nodded.

"Do you come here of your own free will and accord, unbiased by improper solicitation of friends, and uninfluenced by any mercenary or other unworthy motive?"

She licked her lips and uttered, "I do."

"Do you come with a preconceived notion of the excellence of our Order, a desire for knowledge, and to make yourself more extensively useful to your fellow men?"

"Yes, I do."

"Will you willingly conform to the established customs and usages of fraternity?" He cleared his throat, and Elizabeth could tell by the change in his voice that he'd turned his head. "Worshipful Master, I am sorry… Words like men and fraternity are used in this oath. Should we proceed?"

"Again, Senior Deacon, we have all discussed the alternatives. Proceed."

Cool sharp metal pressed against the top of Elizabeth's breast It was an ancient poniard: small, slim, and sharp. One thrust, and it would slide through her skin and straight for her heart.

"Do you feel anything?"

"Y-yes," her voice shook.

"It is the point of a dagger," Arundel spoke softly,

and she wondered if he was secretly enjoying this. "As this pricks your flesh, so may your conscience remember this prick anytime you may be tempted to betray the trust we are now about to place in you."

Sharp pain pierced Elizabeth's skin, making her breath hitch. She didn't dare move, letting the blade caress the delicate flesh. The blade left a burning trail in its wake, and she felt the hot blood seep out to slide down her skin.

"Now, please, Elizabeth, cup your right hand over the wound. This is to remind you that should you betray us, you could have your left breast torn open and your heart plucked out, to be given to the wild beasts of the field and the fowls of the air."

An image of a crow pecking at what remained of her bloody ripped-out heart floated across Elizabeth's mind as she swallowed, feeling ill. The blade fell from her chest as she let out her breath, placing the fingers of her right hand over the stinging cut he'd carved into her. Unlike her brother, the blood didn't continuously flow. Already, it was beginning to clot beneath her fingertips. It stung as she touched it.

"Worshipful Master," said Arundel. "The candidate has been received according to ancient custom."

"Let he who puts his trust in God follow his conductor, fearing no evil," said her father, his voice solemn.

Richard's warm hand enveloped her left one, and he gently led her to another part of the room.

"Kneel."

Her knees touched a pillow as she crouched. The blindfold disorientated her, and she was glad of his guidance.

"Worshipful Master, the candidate is now in the proper position to take the obligation."

"Elizabeth," said her father. Though she was blind, Bizzie could imagine the men around her, well-dressed and faces serious, their thoughts their own. "As we are now about to communicate to you the secrets particular to this degree, the entered apprentice, we require you to take a vow of secrecy. We assure you that everyone here has already taken this oath. Are you willing to take this obligation and by it, become bound to us, as we are to one another?"

What happens if I say no? "I am."

"Since only the free can take a voluntary obligation, I now symbolically release you."

The weight of the rope about her neck lessened as her father's familiar, careful hands uncoiled two of the three coils, lifting most of the weight. The last loop was left hanging about her neck.

"Tonight, you have symbolically escaped two great dangers: strangulation and stabbing." *And being killed by my family*, Elizabeth privately thought but said nothing. "Brother Senior Deacon, your poniard, please."

Warm fingers guided her right hand, wiping off the blood with a rag.

Lord Doneraile pressed the pointed tip of the dagger against his daughter's chest again, just above the wound. He didn't pierce her flesh, but she felt the sharp point against her skin.

"This knife was presented to your left breast. Had you attempted to move forward, you would have caused your own death by stabbing, as the brother who held it would have remained firm and done his duty."

The cold way in which her father uttered the words made Elizabeth swallow, the cold steel pressing on her skin. *If I leaned forward now, the blade would pierce my heart, and they'd feel no guilt.*

"Likewise, with this cable tow," said Lord Doneraile, and she heard the slither of rope as he picked up the cable tow from the ground, "It is to remind you to be mindful of your limitations as a human being. With a noose about your neck, any attempt to run and retreat would have proven fatal." Elizabeth nodded in understanding.

"The other dangers which could await you are what you heard spoken about earlier tonight. Death by throat cutting or drowning—deaths which have befallen traitors before."

Elizabeth thought of the old butler, Mr. Casserly. She imagined the men around her organizing his swift and brutal death. She fought the shiver threatening to wrack her body.

"By spying on us, you learned why it is integral that we keep others in the dark," said Lord Doneraile. "And now, having yourself been for some time in a state of darkness, what do you most stand in need of right now?"

Her immediate thought was a chamber pot, but that wasn't the answer her father was looking for. She wanted to see, to gaze around the room she'd longed to set her eyes upon for so long.

The word flew from Elizabeth's mouth as a croak. "Light."

"And God said, 'Let there be light.'" It sounded like her father was smiling. "And there was light."

Richard took off her blindfold, and Elizabeth

blinked in the new brightness.

Chapter 27

THE ENTERED APPRENTICE

November 1712

Elizabeth knelt before the small oval table with the three candles. Before her was an open Bible, the edges of its pages faded to yellow, the ink faded in spots. A square and compasses sat in the center, forming the shape of a diamond. On the black and white checked floor were two rectangular blocks of stone. One was polished smooth and gleaming. The other was chipped and rough. The ceiling was painted with the directions, north, south east and west.

Her father sat before her in a high-back cedar chair. It had a wooden canopy with its inside ceiling painted like the night sky—dark blue with golden stars. It looked like a throne. Behind it was the ruined wall leading to the library that Mick, the gardener, had burst through earlier.

Elizabeth's brothers surrounded the Worshipful Master, along with Isaac Rothery and Arundel Hill, all with serious expressions. She swallowed. These men had voted to kill her moments before. What were they thinking about all this now?

Lord Doneraile got up and approached his daughter. "Elizabeth Howard St Leger, you are guilty of a crime that should have cost you your life. Apologizing should not have worked here tonight. But these men have chosen to absolve you and make you one of our own."

One man has, Elizabeth thought, bristling. If it weren't for the lifeline Richard had thrown her, she'd have her throat cut by now, be hanging from a noose, or buried with the river water rushing over her head, a snack for the crows. The thought made her want to run.

She looked down at herself, where the cut on her chest had stopped bleeding and was already beginning to scab. The man's shirt hung loose on her frame over her dress.

"Masonry is founded on the purest principles of piety and virtue. It possesses many great and invaluable privileges, and for we trustworthy men alone," her father continued, "vows of fidelity are required. Are you ready to take a great and solemn obligation to keep the secrets and mysteries of the Order?"

A spark of excitement ignited in her heart. "I

208

am."

"Then kneel on your left knee and with your right leg form a square," her father said, pointing at the L-shaped mason's tool before her.

Elizabeth did as she was told, shifting uncomfortably in the unfamiliar garb as she knelt as gracefully as she could manage.

"Give me your right hand, which I place on this book, the *Volume of Sacred Law*. With your left hand, take this compass and present its point to your naked breast."

She placed the point of the compass not far from the wound with her left hand and looked down at her right hand on her father's book. Remnants of dried blood were still under her fingernails.

"Repeat after me," said her father. "In the presence of the Great Architect of the Universe, I do solemnly and sincerely swear that I will always conceal, and never reveal, the hidden points, secrets or mysteries of or belonging to the Ancient Craft of Masonry."

Elizabeth repeated the words, her voice low.

"I will not communicate or divulge these secrets to anyone in the whole world except to other Freemasons, whom after strict examination I determine to be a brother."

She spoke each word as she heard it like a shadow, feeling the men's silent gazes upon her.

"I will not write or print or in any way delineate those secrets on anything moveable or immovable beneath the canopy of heaven. I will not leave any letter or character or symbol, not even the least trace that may be legible to myself of anyone else in the whole world through my negligence or misconduct."

Elizabeth's voice grew stronger as she spoke the vow, though the beginnings of pins and needles were starting to prickle in her legs.

"All these points I solemnly promise, vow, and declare that I will observe without evasion, bearing in mind the ancient penalty of having my throat cut across, my tongue torn out, or my head buried in the sand at low tide. I bind myself under the real penalty of being branded a wretch, faithless, and unworthy to be received by men of honor should I violate in letter or spirit my most sincere obligation as an Entered Apprentice Freemason."

Elizabeth spoke the words, slowly and deliberately, and when she finished, her father gave a slow, satisfied nod.

Chapter 28

SECRET SIGNS AND HANDSHAKES

November 1712

"Is that it?" asked Elizabeth as she put down the compass, removing her hand from the *Volume of Sacred Law.*

Her father laughed as her brothers exchanged smirks. "Far from it, Elizabeth. There are several degrees in Freemasonry, with secrets imparted to each. We will tell you some tonight, but not all. They are conferred upon candidates based on merit, and you must earn the knowledge. I'll entrust you with the secrets of this degree, those marks by how we know each other, distinguished from the rest of the world."

Elizabeth wasn't sure she understood, but she listened with polite respect, wondering when it would be acceptable to cover her shoulder.

"Now stand."

She obeyed, her skirt whispering about her ankles, her left leg still bared from the knee down.

"Take a single step toward me with your left

foot, placing the heel of the right into its hollow."

John stepped forward as she did so. "That is the first regular step in Freemasonry, and it is in this position that the secrets of the degree are communicated," said her brother. "They consist of a due guard, a sign, and a word. This is the due guard. Please copy me."

John stood facing her and placed his left hand, palm facing up, at his abdomen. He then covered it with his right hand facing down.

"This is to remind you of the oath you just took on the *Volume of Sacred Law*, with your left hand supporting it and your right hand resting on it."

Elizabeth mirrored her brother. He gave her a small smile, then took a seat as Hayes got to his feet, his reddish locks glowing in the lantern light.

"Now I will teach you the sign," said Hayes. "Copy me."

Hayes lifted his right hand to the left of his own throat, extended his thumb to make a right angle, and drew it sharply across his neck. Elizabeth mirrored him, fighting off the shiver that longed to crawl across her shoulders.

Her father explained, "As you can probably guess, this sign represents the penalty of divulging secrets. A brother would rather his throat cut out than flap his mouth about the secrets of Freemasonry."

Elizabeth swallowed, nodding.

"Now, I will teach you myself the grip of the Entered Apprentice," said Lord Doneraile. "Give me your hand."

Elizabeth extended her right hand to her father. When his hand took hers, he placed his thumb on the knuckle of her forefinger and applied enough pressure where she felt it.

"This is the grip of the Entered Apprentice, and it serves to help you distinguish another brother by night or by day."

Elizabeth nodded, but her father did not let go of her hand.

"Once upon a time, these signs and grips were used to get important men out of harm's way. Men without whom you and I would not be here today. They were the Knights Templar."

Elizabeth was familiar with the Knights Templar and the Crusades, and her ancestors' involvement. Theirs were stories told to her as a child.

"When the order was disbanded four hundred years ago, the Knights Templar and the secrets they learned on their missions in the Holy Land were protected by men like us, Freemasons. This grip was one way they escaped burning at the stake by posing as stone masons working on the great cathedrals of Europe and knowing whom to trust by these signs and handshakes.

"This grip comes with a word, a word that traces directly back to the great architect who designed King Solomon's temple. The word is used to safeguard our privileges, and one cannot use too much caution when deciding when and where to use it." Her father leaned down and whispered in her ear. She thought she misheard him.

Elizabeth looked quizzically into her father's eyes.

"Bo-what?" she whispered, trying to communicate privately with him before he pulled away to stand upright again.

"Silence!" he shouted, towering over her. "Never are you ever to say that word aloud!"

Lord Doneraile's patience was wearing thin as his embarrassment grew…the unfinished wall, his book found left out, yet another disloyal butler and this disobedient daughter now before him. He couldn't allow her to say the word out loud on top of it all!

"You heard me. It is a word like none other in our language. And should you need to use it, only a fellow Freemason will know how. Brother Rothery, will you please?"

Isaac stood before Lord Doneraile, several inches shorter than the older man. The two shook hands, each placing a thumb upon the other's first knuckle, just as she was just instructed.

"What does the grip demand?" asked Lord Doneraile.

"A word," said Isaac.

"Give me that word."

"At my initiation, I was taught to be cautious, but I will letter or halve it with you."

"Letter it, and you begin."

"A."

"B."

"O."

"Z."

Puzzled, Elizabeth silently repeated in her mind the two syllables her father had just whispered to her.

"But that can't be the correct spelling," Elizabeth said out loud, her voice coming out high-pitched and soft compared to the men around her. She cleared her throat as elegantly as she could.

"Yes," said her father. "Only a Freemason would know that my dear."

"What does it mean?"

Lord Doneraile let go of Isaac's hand and took his seat. "As my daughter, you've heard my countless tales of the great King Solomon."

She nodded, recalling the day he'd told her of King Solomon's son and the third egg.

"Two great pillars once stood at the porch of King Solomon's temple in Jerusalem, the one that was destroyed long before the birth of Jesus. It was designed by a talented man from the city of Tyre named Hiram Abiff. One of the pillars was called the word you just heard, which is actually a name. It is named after King David's great-grandfather."

"What was the other one called?" asked Elizabeth.

"The other?"

"The other pillar. You said there were two."

Lord Doneraile smiled as all the men shifted around her, silent and watchful. "That, my dear, is a secret for another time."

Chapter 29

THE ROUGH ASHLAR

November 1712

The sun would surely be rising by now. Her body ached from a night with no sleep, and she longed to crawl into her bed, but her father was not yet finished.

"Elizabeth, you are now what we call an Entered Apprentice. You may be wondering what that means, and an apprentice of what? You may have heard we call ourselves Masons, but as you may have already guessed, we do not take part in the manual labor of an operative mason. Nor shall you."

Lord Doneraile gestured to the two blocks of stone, which he now stood beside. One of them was large and jagged, the other chiseled and polished to a high shine. "You are like this undressed stone," he said, his long fingers pointing toward the rough ashlar. "By joining us, you join our quest to be like this smooth, polished stone, the perfect ashlar. That is where your tools come in." He pointed to the wooden pedestal before her, holding the Bible, the candles, and the compass.

"We use certain implements of operative masonry to impress upon us moral lessons. These are the working tools of the Entered Apprentice Degree." The other men brought the tools over, placing them onto the pedestal as he spoke.

"We have here a gavel, a trowel, a gauge, the compass, a plumb, and a square. The twenty-four-inch gauge is divided by marks into twenty-four equal parts. The operative mason uses it to bring his work to the required dimensions. We have adopted it to represent the twenty-four hours in a day. It reminds us to divide our time in daily life between our vocations, rest, and recreation, but also in service to our Creator. It is to be a symbol of time well spent."

Elizabeth examined the tools as her father introduced them.

"The gavel is used by the operative mason to knock off the corners of the rough stone so it fits better, more cleanly. We have adopted it to remind us of divesting our minds and consciences of all the vices and impurities of life."

"And what of the rest?" she asked.

"Those are also tools for another lesson. Now

218

come to me."

Elizabeth approached her father, the Worshipful Master. He took off his apron and tied it around her.

"This is to protect you from rough stones and tools. It is white leather made from lambskin." His blue eyes met hers. "A symbol of innocence."

Chapter 30

THE CORNERSTONE

November 1712

The early morning sun now peeked through the slats of the wooden shutters covering the windows of the paneled room. Elizabeth stifled a yawn by clamping her lips together, her eyes watering from the effort. It felt unnatural to still be awake, and it felt like a thousand years had passed since she'd crouched by the bricks to spy on the Lodge meeting the night before. How had it been only hours since she'd sneaked beneath that white sheet and into the pendulum clock that had ultimately gotten her caught?

"Brother Aldworth," said Lord Doneraile, "please now take Brother – or is it Sister? Oh, we will have to figure this out later, won't we?" The men all laughed in a needed release of tension from the past night. "Brother Aldworth, please take Elizabeth to the northeast corner."

Richard led Elizabeth to the corner; the cardinal directions painted on the ceiling spelled out where to go. The ghost of his kiss was still on her lips, and her heart raced as she felt his warmth beside her.

"Elizabeth Howard St. Leger, we place you now in the northeast corner of this room as the cornerstone of your life in Freemasonry has been laid," her father said. "You have gone through the ceremony of initiation. You are now a member of our ancient and honorable society. You now embody principles that have existed from time immemorial, principles that have been passed down generation to generation and celebrated here within the confines of our brotherhood. I congratulate you on this achievement, but your trials are not yet over. You have been entered. You still need to be passed and raised."

Elizabeth waited as the men all watched her. Finally, she said, "What does that mean?"

Richard's soft voice said, "In due course, you shall know."

"I hereby close this Lodge with the words that have been passed down to us," Lord Doneraile said to the group, who all responded in unison, "*Mat ne menal mat bal.*"

"Well, what does that mean?" Elizabeth whispered to Richard.

He shrugged. "No one knows."

Intrigued by another mystery to be solved, she repeated the words as best she could.

Chapter 31

THE NEXT DAY

November 1712

As the sun rose, casting its orange glow on the world, Richard and Elizabeth opened the front door of Doneraile Court and walked out, the cold breeze rippling their clothes and hair, making Elizabeth feel a little more awake. She had finally been allowed to take off that men's shirt and had pulled a shawl over her shoulders, but not before pressing a small bandage to the wound on her chest, hoping it would not scar.

Richard smiled at her, his hazel eyes crinkling. She found herself smiling back as he took her cold small hand in his warm large one. She could feel he was still wearing the golden ring he'd taken from her. His warmth entwined in her fingers, they headed for Fishpond Lane. It was pleasant to revel in the silence of the early morning, to hear the twitter of birds and the gurgle of the stream.

The town, when they reached it, was in uproar.

"It was a banshee!" Mrs. Kelly cried, her latest

infant clutched to her chest as she waddled up and down the marketplace, calling out to anyone who would listen. "A banshee, I tell you! Nothing's made such a terrifying sound as that in all my long years!"

Shoppers and passers-by mostly ignored her ramblings, though the word "banshee" struck fear into their hearts, especially as she spoke with such determined fear.

The townspeople didn't notice the only daughter of Lord Doneraile gliding past them, her gown cut off at the knees, her hair disheveled from no sleep, and holding the hand of a stranger.

Elizabeth and Richard passed the bakery, where the sweet scent of early morning pastries and bread floated through the air. Mrs. O'Beirne and Mrs. O'Keeffe were lined up outside the building, whispering about how everyone in their house was accounted for and crossing themselves. The morning was marred by panic and confusion, superstitious hysteria making waves around town of monsters and ghouls.

"It certainly wasn't a banshee, though. We know that," she whispered to Richard.

"Too bad you can't tell these people that," Richard whispered back, chuckling.

Their oaths of secrecy meant the people of Doneraile would need to have faith that the screaming banshee passed them over—for now, at least.

"They aren't entirely wrong, though," she declared. "Someone did die last night. And someone else was born."

She was not thinking of William's final ragged gasp or Brigid's baby's first burst of tears, but of her own place on earth. The girl called Bizzie was gone. A stronger, wiser woman named Elizabeth now stood.

Today, I am a better than yesterday, she thought, linking her arm in Richard's elbow.

But not as good as I hope to be tomorrow.

\#

Epilogue

"Elizabeth St. Leger Aldworth"
Courtesy of Freemasons' Hall, Cork

The real Elizabeth St. Leger was initiated into

the mysteries of Freemasonry in November 1712. Records show there was a full moon on November 13th of that year.

Elizabeth actually received two degrees that first night, Entered Apprentice and Fellowcraft, which was the custom at the time. She married Richard Aldworth five months later, in April 1713, and became the Honorable Elizabeth Aldworth. They lived together as husband and wife, active Freemasons, and passionate philanthropists for nearly sixty years.

Doneraile Court, the house where her initiation

Courtesy: Maureen O'Hanlon

took place, is still standing after extensive renovations spanning the past five decades. A portrait of Elizabeth hangs there in the library. The house and its surrounding wildlife preserve are open to the public as they are owned by the state and operated by Ireland's Office of Public Works. Doneraile Estate is one of the top tourist attractions in Cork County.

If you visit, you will find the house much changed since the days surrounding Elizabeth's initiation. Sometime in the 1720s-1730s, Doneraile Court was renovated by Isaac Rothery, the same architect who built Newmarket Court for the Aldworths. The rounded bows on either side were added after a fire sometime around 1805, and the front portico sometime after that.

A floor plan from the time of Elizabeth's

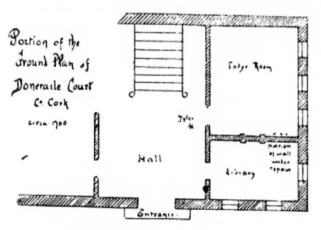

Courtesy: Memoir of The Lady Freemason

initiation shows a smaller footprint with no bows, no portico. The room behind the library is clearly marked "Lodge Room" and on the wall between them an area is marked "portion of wall under repair."

Despite the extraordinary circumstances surrounding her impromptu initiation, Elizabeth embraced and venerated Freemasonry. She went on to become a Master Mason and remained active in the society as it evolved over her lifetime. She was even spotted wearing her full Masonic regalia publicly in an open carriage during processions.

It is said she would never allow Freemasonry to be "spoken lightly of" in her presence and was careful not to talk about it in front of any non-Masons. She was known as The Lady Freemason.

When she died around age eighty, the following obituary was published in the *Limerick Chronicle*:

On Monday last, died, in Newmarket, in this county, the Hon. Mrs Elizabeth Aldworth, wife of Richard Aldworth, Esq., M.P. She lived to the age of eighty, and such were the effects of her early education, under the good Lord Doneraile, her father, and her own happy disposition, that from her infancy, perhaps, there passed not a day which might not have been distinguished by some one act of her benevolence or charity. She lived, for the most part of her time, in the country, and in the midst of her tenants, to whom her house afforded the most cheerful hospitality; the meanest of them, when their wants required it, had access to her, and when the indigent sick called on her, she never failed to dispense her favors with that bounty and humanity which a large fortune enabled her, and a still larger soul induced her to bestow. Indeed, Heaven seemed to have appointed her the guardian of the poor, whom she relieved without ostentation.

Elizabeth Aldworth received a full Masonic funeral. She was laid to rest beneath Saint Fin Barre's Cathedral in Cork City in County Cork, Ireland.

About one hundred years later, her coffin was opened during construction of the current cathedral. A fellow Freemason observed her body and reported finding her perfectly preserved. He describes her appearance a century after her death in a memoir published by her family in 1811:

> She was in a leaden shell and in a wonderful state of preservation. She was attired in a dark silk dress, white satin shoes and silk stockings of a similar colour. Her person was comely; her face of a dusky or ash colour; her features quite perfect and calm. She had long silk gloves, which extended above the embroidered lace wrist-bands; her bosom was full and large for her age; she wore a white head-dress with a full frill around her neck the plaits of which were not even ruffled.

She was reinterred under the present cathedral, and a brass plaque there honors her life in Freemasonry.

Today, there are thousands of active female Freemasons in offshoot organizations around the world. One of them, Le Droit Humain, named its first lodge after her.

However, the Honorable Elizabeth Aldworth remains the first and only female Freemason recognized in Ireland as a member of the regular, all-male fraternity. Her portrait hangs in the Grand Lodge in Dublin and at Freemasons' Hall in Cork.

The Freemasons' Hall in Cork maintains a small museum dedicated to The Lady Freemason, complete with her apron, marriage certificate, and other personal items donated by her family.

Elizabeth and Richard Aldworth
Courtesy: Ben Stocks

About the Author

Kathleen Aldworth Foster is a veteran journalist and television news producer who spent 25 years covering major breaking news events, including 9/11, the wars in Iraq & Afghanistan, and interviewing heads of state around the world. This is her first novel. Kathleen is a lifelong lover of travel, history, and old houses. She and her husband Chris live in New Jersey with their twin daughters, Elizabeth and Mary.

Resources

Memoir of The Lady Freemason – *multiple editions* – Brother John Day
The Aldworth Papers – Cork City & County Archives
Aldworth/Elbridge Genealogical and Biographical Monographs – Edward Elbridge Salisbury
The Aldworth Women – Raymond O'Sullivan
Corkpastandpresent.ie
Doneraile land deeds
Haunted Chambers – The Lives of Early Women Freemasons - Karen Kidd
The Poison Garden at Blarney Castle
The Mallow Field Club Journal – Mallow Archeological & Historical Society
Plantation McAuliffe & Newmarket Court – IRD Dunhallow/ James O'Keeffe Institute
Doneraile Forest Park Pamphlet
Auction List of Doneraile Court Library – Hamilton & Hamilton Estates Limited
A Taste of Doneraile - Michael O'Sullivan
Donerailecourt.ie
A System of Speculative Masonry: Course of Lectures – Grand Chapter of the State of NY 1822

The Hiram Key – Christopher Knight & Robert Lomas

The Hiram Key Revisited – Christopher Knight & Alan Butler

St. Leger: The Family and The Race – Moya Frenz St. Leger

The Early Masonic Catechisms – Knoop, Jones and Hamer

Freemasons' Guide and Compendium – Bernard E. Jones

Born in Blood – John J. Robinson

Synan Family Historical Society – Synan.org

A Gentlemen's Village: Seats & Estates of Doneraile – Anna Maria Hajba lecture

Colonial Foodways of the 1600s – Patricia B. Mitchell

Words They Lived By – Joan P. Bines

The Arcane Schools – John Yarker

The Book that Jesus Wrote – Barbara Thiering

The Secret Legacy of Jesus – Jeffrey J. Butz

Secret Traditions in Freemasonry – Arthur Edward Watte

Duncan's Masonic Ritual and Monitor – Malcolm C. Duncan

Irish Ritual of Craft – Freemasonry as Worked Under Warrant of the GL of Ireland – Anonymous

Irishmasonichistory.com

The Hon Miss St. Leger and Freemasonry – Bro
Edward Conder

*Custodians of Truth: The Continuance of Rex
Deus*- Tim Wallace Murphy and Marilyn Hopkins

Level Steps – Jonti Marks

Making Good Men Better – Carl W. Davis

Masonic Words & Phrases – Michael R. Poll

Masonic Enlightenment – Michael R. Poll

Look to the East – Ralph P. Lester

The Craft – John Dickie

Sworn in Secret – Sanford Holst

Caribbean – James A. Michener

Ireland – Frank Delaney

The True & Exact History of Barbados – Richard
Ligon

The Enlightened – Manly P. Hall

To Hell or Barbados – Sean O'Callaghan

Library of Barbados Museum and Historical
Society Records

*The Signet of King Solomon; or The Freemason's
Daughter* – Augustus C.L. Arnold

101 Secrets of the Freemasons – Barb Karg and
John K. Young

The Bible

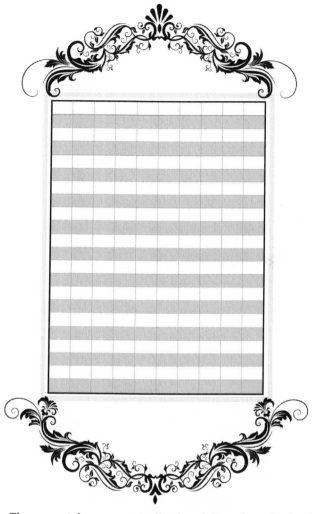

There are ciphers strategically placed throughout this book.
Decode the message to find out
WHO KILLED MR. CASSERLY.
Go to DoneraileCourt.com to see the
MASON'S CIPHER KEY
and SOLVE THE MYSTERY. Use this grid to write down the
characters in order of appearance. Leave a space when you see
a blank page. A printable PDF of this grid is also available at
DoneraileCourt.com